HOLLY ISLAND

S J CRABB

MORE BOOKS BY S J CRABB

sjcrabb.com

PROLOGUE

The door opens and an icy blast causes me to shiver. The small heater underneath the counter does little to warm the chill in the air as I shuffle a little closer to it.

Once again, I stare at the advert on my phone that appears to taunt me every time I see it. Holly Island.

To me, it sounds like paradise and I can't think of anything I want more than to escape there.

"Excuse me."

Looking up, I see the vacant stare of a customer glancing around her in confusion and I smile warmly, which quite frankly is the only warmth on offer in this decrepit, dusty bookshop.

"How may I help you?"

She looks worried and a little flustered, which is usual at this time of year, as shoppers contemplate the mammoth task ahead of them as they struggle to work their way through their Xmas shopping list.

"I need a book for my nephew. What do you recommend?"

Sighing inside, I try to look anything but irritated as I say kindly, "How old is he?"

"I don't know," she shrugs, as if it's of no consequence.

I take a deep breath. "A guess then."

"Maybe nine, then again, he could be ten, or even eleven. Come to think of it, he could be six. They look older than they are these days."

I smile again and wonder if there are medals available for dealing with clueless people on a daily basis because, if there are, I deserve a gold one.

I press on. "Do you know what he likes?"

The look she shoots me pre-warns me of her answer as she shrugs again.

"No, I've never met him."

"Oh."

"Well, he lives in Australia, and this is his first visit. To be honest, it's a bit inconvenient, really. I mean, there are four of them and I've never met them, but my sister wants the whole family around on Christmas Day to show off her amazing Antipodean family. Obviously, Roger and I would much rather stay at home with a ready meal for two, but what can you say? Now I have the added expense of four more presents and the trouble of taking some flowers and stuff. You know, Christmas is getting out of hand and I can't wait for it to be over."

"What about Harry Potter?"

"Harry who, I don't think he's on the guest list?"

"No, Harry Potter - the book. I'm sure he would love that."

She looks thoughtful. "Isn't that encouraging witchcraft and the occult? I think it was banned from the village library and I don't want to corrupt his young mind."

My patience is fast deserting me as I wave towards the bookcase by the door. "Why don't you take a look at the teen fiction? Maybe something there will catch your eye."

She looks at me as if I've suggested she run for Prime Minister and says quickly, "I wouldn't know where to start. No, just choose one for me and make sure that it's under £5 because it's not as if I'll ever see them again."

Sighing, I venture out from the only warm spot in the entire shop and brave the chill to grab the nearest book, while stifling the words that threaten to tell the woman exactly what I think of her. However, she is typical of the people who come into the shop at this time of year. Clueless!

The sooner I get rid of her, the better because I want to study that advert a little longer and dream the impossible dream because Holly Island is just that. A dream that would take me away from my reality.

I place the book in a brown paper bag and say quickly, "That will be 4.99, please?"

She starts to fumble in her bag and I wait patiently as she sighs, "Bloody bag. Ever since they started charging for carriers, I've had to use the biggest shopping bag I can find. Now I can't find anything I need - do you mind?"

I shake my head as she proceeds to empty her bag onto the floor as she looks for her purse and my mind wanders back to Holly Island. I'm pretty certain everything is perfect there. It says so in the advert, so it must be true.

"Found it."

She holds her purse up triumphantly, and I smile wearily. "Great."

She spends the next five minutes counting out the correct money in 5p pieces and laughs. "Sorry about this. I save them up and they help with the Christmas shopping. I must have saved about £30 this year; it's such a good idea."

As she counts, the phone rings and I grab it eagerly before I am tempted to scream.

"Bibbidy, Bobbidy, Bookshop, how may I help you?"

"Hello, Scarlett, are you busy?

My heart sinks. "Hi Gregory, yes I am as it happens."

"Oh, ok, I won't keep you long then. I just wanted to check if you were still ok to meet on Saturday."

Inwardly, I roll my eyes. "Of course, but that is still two days from now."

There's a slight pause and I note a hint of uncertainty in his voice as he says, "I just wanted to make sure; I don't want anything to go wrong."

The warning bells ring loud and clear as the customer smiles triumphantly. "Here you go, I think you'll find the exact amount."

Grateful for the distraction, I say quickly, "I've got to go, Gregory, I have a customer."

Before he can speak, I disconnect the call and try to push away the thought of what I think is coming as I start to count the large pile of coins on the counter.

I'm just grateful for the distraction because my heart is sinking quicker than a brick in quicksand as I contemplate the reason for Gregory's call.

Thrusting the paper bag to the customer, I say quickly, "Thank you, um... Happy Christmas."

Then, without waiting for a reply, I disappear into the stock room and take a few deep zen breaths to restore my inner calm.

The tears smart behind my eyes and I try desperately to think of something to distract me from the impending date with Gregory. I'm not silly and know what his intentions are. He's not that good at hiding things and if I'm not mistaken, a proposal is heading my way like a tsunami and will be every bit as devastating.

I hear the door chime and turn my attention back to the reason I'm here. Business.

I have worked in Bibbidy Bobbidy for three years now and most of the time love my job. Mr Saracen is a lovely man who leaves me to run his shop without any intervention most of the time. I get to surround myself in a world of fiction rather than face the reality of my empty life and just absorb the words of the many books on offer as they take me to places I've only ever dreamed of going.

"Scarlett, are you in there?"

My heart lifts as I recognise my friend Rita's voice and head out to greet her.

"Honestly, Scarlett, I don't know how you don't catch pneumonia stuck in here for most of the day. Is there no heating at all in this place?"

"Sadly no. The budget won't stretch to central heating. It's a fridge in winter and a sauna in the summer."

"Well, I'd start looking for alternative employment if I were you. Surely there are rules about this kind of thing in the European directives."

"I'm sure there are, but Mr Saracen lives and works by his own rules and nothing will ever change that."

She looks around her with a critical eye and says wearily, "You know, you're wasted here. Why don't you make it your New Year's resolution to change direction? You're an intelligent woman and could work anywhere and be good at it. Why do you insist on burying yourself here?"

"Because it's easy, I suppose. It's close to home. I save money on travel expenses and I'm my own boss most of the time. I love it to be honest and wouldn't get the same job satisfaction anywhere else."

"Rubbish! Look at me, for example. I'm doing really well on the cosmetics counter at Selfridges. I'm mixing with the elite and living the dream; I earn more than you, minus the travel expenses and get a great staff discount. I meet so many interesting people and am inundated with offers from gorgeous men. That could be you if you only shrugged off that old, moth-eaten cardigan and embraced your inner vixen. I mean, when was the last time you went to the hair-dressers and got your hair styled? When was the last time you had a makeover and actually bought some fashionable clothes? It's criminal the way you present yourself to the world because underneath all that drudgery is a sex symbol screaming to get out."

We grin at each other, and then I sigh wearily again. "I think Gregory's going to propose."

Rita's eyes widen in horror and she whispers, "You poor thing; what are you going to say?"

I shrug and she squeals, "You're not actually thinking of saying yes, are you? Please tell me you're not! I mean, for goodness' sake, Scarlett, this charade has gone on long enough; you have got to end it with him."

I lean on the counter and groan. "How can I? It would break his heart?"

Rita looks at me so ferociously I feel afraid for my life as she says angrily, "Then he will have to learn to get over it. This has gone on long enough and you need to set you both free to find someone else. I mean, how could you possibly even consider accepting a marriage proposal from a man who thinks a membership to the caravan club would make a good Christmas present?"

"It wasn't so bad. Just because we didn't actually have a caravan, it was the thought that counted."

Rita snorts. "I'm sorry, but a couple of sleeping bags thrown in the back of a Volvo estate do not constitute a caravan."

"We were trying it out to see if it was something we would enjoy, and as Gregory said, the best campsites are restricted to the members of the caravan club. They have electricity and showers and are, quite honestly, a home from home."

The sound of Rita's foot tapping angrily on the wooden floor indicates her disapproval far more than words as she raises her eyes and says quickly, "What about the matching jumpers he made you wear last Christmas when he signed you up for carol singing at the local hospice? What about the trip to Blackpool he arranged in the Air B&B that was obviously run by a psychopath and what about the year he enrolled you both in an evening class learning Chinese because he thought it would give you a head start in life? For god's sake, the man's a liability and not in the real world. Where are the romantic dinners and trips abroad to an all-inclusive paradise? Where are the flowers and chocolates and ribbon wrapped packages in interesting designer bags?"

She holds up her hand and says firmly, "Nando's does not count as fine dining, so do yourself a huge favour and ditch the loser."

I know I should defend Gregory, be angry at the way she speaks of him and firmly put her in her place by declaring my undying love for my boyfriend of the last five years, but I can't. Gregory Richardson is everything she described and more. We are poles apart and it's obvious to everyone, but him, it seems. The trouble is, he was my first everything. My first kiss, my first exploration past the layers of practical clothing we always wear and my first boyfriend. The last thing I want to be is his first heartbreak, but then again, if I stay, it will break my heart and I'm not sure what to do about it.

Rita throws me a pitying look and says firmly, "You do know I'm right, don't you?"

I nod miserably and she smiles reassuringly. "Be brave and end it. Make next year the year of the Scarlett woman. Give your life a makeover and reach for the stars. Don't hold back because there is no rewind button in life. You owe it to yourself to live the best life you can because nobody else will do it for you. Don't take the safe road in life and don't rely on anyone else because you, Madame, are invincible."

She looks at her phone and smiles ruefully. "Sorry, I've got to get a move on. Unlike some, I have a hair appointment and this close to Christmas they're like gold dust."

She turns away and then says over her shoulder, "Remember what I said and ditch him. It will be hard at first, but I'm guessing as soon as you're free of him you'll feel as if a weight has lifted."

As I watch her leave, I think back to Holly Island. Reaching for my phone, I scroll through Facebook until I find the ever-present advert.

Yes, Holly Island could be the answer to everything and so, before I can change my mind, I click on the Ad and before I know what's happening, just a few clicks is all it takes to book myself on the next available date - tomorrow.

I can't believe I did it.

I actually did it.

I left home and here I am. All it took was a taxi ride to the airport, a short flight, and another taxi to the ferry port. I say port, more like a jetty, but I. Did. It.

So what if Mr Saracen was inconvenienced when I called him and told him I quit? So what if my mother screamed at me on the phone that Christmas was ruined forever because she would now be two down around the Christmas table? So what if my bank balance took a major hit? It's not as if the savings were earning much interest, anyway. I suppose it was just lucky that I saved most of my money because I have enough to tide me over for a few months while I look for a new job when I return.

No, I was impetuous, reckless and inconsiderate and I couldn't care less because once I get to Holly Island my dreams will come true.

Purposefully, I don't think about what Gregory will think when he receives the Christmas card that I posted yesterday explaining my need to escape and think about the direction my life is taking. I try not to picture the pain and disappointment on his face as his date is scuppered. I only think about the new adventure heading my way and the screams of delight from my friend as I called Rita and told her of my plans. Yes, she was right. This is what I need to do and when Christmas is over and I head home, I will be reborn.

The air is still, and the fog is rolling in and I pull my oversized padded coat a little tighter. The fur-lined boots I'm wearing are doing a bad job of keeping my toes from freezing and I shift from one foot to the other to try to restore the circulation. The gloves with hand warmer inserts are battling the elements as the breath from my body freezes as it hits the air outside. It's cold. So cold I wonder if this was such a good idea. Looking around, I see nobody else waiting and wonder if I've come to the right place. Surely there should be more guests waiting to enjoy a dream Christmas?

Only the call of the bird's overhead and the gentle lapping of the waves indicate another form of life as I wait for the ferry to take me to paradise.

It feels quite eerie as I wait and I try to stifle the feeling of unease that is fast gaining the upper hand inside me. Maybe I got the last place and everyone else is already there. That must be right, because this close to Christmas it was sure to have sold out ages ago.

I hear the gentle splash of someone approaching and just make out a dim light heading towards me through the fog. My heart starts beating faster as I think back to the books I read and wonder if the man's a murderer in disguise or a vampire. He could be a ghost who haunts the waters, or an axe murderer. My life may end on that sinister water and everyone will remember me as the foolhardy woman with her head in the clouds who dared to dream.

I stifle a shriek as the boat draws nearer and I make out a huddled figure rowing to shore. I hold my breath as he pulls alongside the jetty and I take my first look at a man that would make Hagrid appear sophisticated.

"Scarlett Robins?"

The voice that asks is thick and deep. There's an accent that I can't quite place and I say nervously, "Yes."

"Is that all your luggage?"

I look at the small wheeled suitcase I brought with me and nod. "Yes."

"Hand it to me."

Trying to get a grip on the handle of my case with ski gloves is proving a little tricky, and it takes me a while to get a grip but I manage to haul the case over the side of the boat and hand it to the surly sailor. Unsure what to do next, I watch as he places it carefully to one side and then nods. "Get in."

Swallowing hard, I edge forward gingerly and worry that the boat is rocking dangerously and looks to have seen better days as he says gruffly, "Hurry up, the tide won't wait for anyone."

Trying to appear as if I do this all the time, I head towards the boat and look for a rail or something to grip onto. Finding nothing, I hesitate and the man makes a clicking noise and holds out his hand to pull me in. As I take the gnarly old hand of what could be a murderer, I find myself being hauled into a rickety old boat and stumble as I almost fall inside.

"Take a seat and hold on tight."

Quickly, I do as he says and then say in a shaky voice, "Um... is there anyone else coming?"

He starts to push us away from the side and says gruffly, "No."

I watch as he fiddles with a small outboard engine and after a few tries, it splutters into life and signifies the end of any conversation.

As we pull away from the shore, the jetty disappears into the fog and not for the first time I wonder if this is it - the end.

The gentle chug of the engine and the bounce of the waves cancel out any conversation as we start the journey to Holly Island. The darkness is rolling in and there is the distinct feeling of rain in the air. The clouds look ominous and I try to calm myself down with images of roaring fires and hot chocolate with marshmallows, waiting for me at my destination.

I'm sure I'll look back on this and laugh at how scared I felt when I chat about my experience with the other guests in the warm, cosy, communal living area. Yes, I'll soon be tucked up with a good book and a mug of something hot, while an amazing meal is prepared for me in the bustling kitchens of the five-star kitchen I was promised.

I almost smile as I think about the treats in store and am carried away by my daydreams before being brought back to reality as a gruff voice says, "Hold on, we're going to pull alongside the jetty."

Quickly, I look around and see we've arrived at last and feel the excitement stirring inside. I'm here. I'm on Holly Island and my life is about to change. I really did it. I threw caution to the wind and took a chance. It's a bold move and completely out of character and I feel a rush of adrenalin as I look with interest at the place I will call home for the next two weeks. I'm here.

CHAPTER 2

*S*omehow, I manage to get out of the boat with my dignity intact. Hauling the suitcase out is another one of life's experiences and my surly companion does nothing to help, other than watch me with mild curiosity.

The wind blows and chills me inside, despite the number of layers that I shrouded myself in, and I shiver. "Is it always this cold?"

He grunts in reply and then says sourly, "Follow the path through the trees. You may want to get a move on, the storm's coming in and you won't want to be caught in it."

I open my mouth to deliver the hundreds of questions inside, but he just pulls away from the jetty and the sound of the outboard engine drowns them out. Great. Stranded on a dark, unforgiving island without so much as a welcoming committee to greet me.

As I turn away from the jetty, I feel a surge of pride that I made it this far at all. I can't believe I did it, it's so unlike me. I have always played safe in my life and this is the most reckless thing I've ever done.

Ignoring the part of me that hates what I've done to Mr

Saracen and Gregory, I start walking up the path towards my bright future.

My feet are so cold they will hardly move and the wheels on the case are hopeless on the rough terrain. Sighing, I try to heave the case up the track and just hope the hotel isn't far because a sudden clap of thunder announces the arrival of a storm that appears to have blown up out of nowhere.

The rain lashes down, soaking me in seconds as the coat I'm wearing demonstrates that you should never buy the cheaper option. The water starts running down my neck, leaving cold, icy fingers trailing down my already freezing skin and promising an uncomfortable journey. My boots prove the waterproof barrier was forgotten to be added as my feet start squelching in time to my footsteps. The warm woollen hat I'm wearing is sodden in seconds as the rain drips down my nose, reminding me that my hands are otherwise occupied with holding onto my worldly possessions.

This place is dark and ominous and I wonder why the owners don't invest in welcoming fairy lights, or festively adorned trees to create a cosy atmosphere and aid progress through the stark landscape.

Lightning crackles overhead and I'm suddenly aware of how exposed I am to a near-death experience as I make my way through the trees. Once again, I berate myself for the impetuous behaviour I have adopted and wonder if I am in danger of losing my sanity.

The walk to the hotel seems interminable as I stumble on as quickly as possible, desperate for a glimpse of a welcome light in a window where a fire beckons, beside which is a steaming mug of hot chocolate with my name on it. Briefly, I imagine the unfavourable review I will post on Trip Advisor at my treatment so far because this is far from any dreams I have ever had. More like a nightmare and I half expect to find Bates' Motel nestling in the trees around the next bend.

Finally, I see the end in sight as I see a large building loom into view and I catch my breath. It looks deserted.

The tears smart behind my eyes as I stare in disbelief at the large house looking anything but welcoming as it stands proudly among the trees. It appears empty due to the fact there is no sign of life at all, and I wonder if I've come to the right place. Maybe this is the lodge house or something along those lines. Perhaps the hotel is further up the path and this is just an unused building. My shoulders sag as I contemplate a further journey up the unwelcome path and then I hear the sound of a door opening and a voice shout loudly, "Hurry up and get inside before you catch pneumonia."

Looking up, I can just about make out a figure standing in the dimly lit entrance and, needing no further invitation, I rush towards him eagerly. So what if he's a mass murderer and I am heading towards my death; it's a small price to pay for escaping the storm?

In a rush, I fall through the door and blink as the light from a torch finds my face, and a voice says gruffly, "Get out of those wet clothes and I'll find you a blanket. I've lit a fire in the snug and there's some tea brewing."

Quickly, I scramble out of my coat and boots and note with dismay the puddle on the floor as they drip all over it. As I raise my eyes, a blanket is thrust at me and I see a man disappearing towards another door across a large hallway. Abandoning my suitcase, I head after him and say loudly, "Excuse me, but is this Holly Island hotel? I think I may be in the wrong place."

I watch as he shakes his head and says angrily, "No, this is the right place but it's far from what you were expecting."

He flings open a large wooden door and I almost cry with happiness as I see a roaring fire dancing in the grate inside and two comfortable chairs positioned in front of it. There are a few candles dotted around the room, which, along with the flames, provide the only light in the room. Then the man says wearily, "The power's down. The storm knocked it out and we have no light or heat. If it doesn't kick in soon, we are in for a cold night. I thought it would be best to stay in one room until things get back to normal."

I follow him inside and note a small room filled with antique furniture and ornate rugs. It looks almost regency in its appearance and I can feel the history surrounding me as I stare in open wonder at a room that wouldn't look out of place in a Jane Austen novel.

My companion pokes the fire and adds another log and then as he turns around, my breath hitches as he is revealed to me for the first time. I did not expect this… him. For once I am speechless and just stare at a man who has obviously escaped from a romance novel. Tall, dark and handsome doesn't do this man justice. Images of Heathcliff and Ross Poldark entwine and I feel my heart rate increase as I take in the slightly long, messy hair, melting, dark brown eyes and a smattering of dark stubble across a clearly defined strong jaw. His mouth is inviting and the arms that hang beside his clearly toned body look as if they could crush an opponent in a matter of seconds.

Inside, I am a mess. A girly puddle of desire as all of my dreams come together and stand before me, looking at me with mild curiosity. It's only when I see the smirk on his face that I realise what a total freaking mess I must look. Self-consciously, I raise my hand to brush the wet hair that is plastered across my cheek away and feel my teeth chatter as much from nerves as the cold as I stare at manly perfection.

Yes, this is a MAN! Every fine inch of him is crafted from women's fantasies and as companions to weather a storm goes - I've hit the jackpot.

Pulling the blanket around my shivering body, I say nervously, "I'm sorry. My name's Scarlett Robins and I've booked the Christmas 'escape it all' package. Am I in the right place?"

He raises his eyes and smiles with amusement, before saying in a deep, sexy voice, "You and me both. It appears that we are the only ones though."

I stare at him in shock and he laughs. "There is nobody else here. I'm not sure where they are, but when I arrived earlier the place was deserted. It appears to be well-stocked and ready for guests, but this place is like the Marie Celeste and we are its only occupants."

I open my mouth but no words follow and he laughs. "Take a seat and make use of the warmth from the fire. I'll fetch us some tea and we can work out what the hell is going on."

He heads off and my mind races out of control. What the…? I can't believe it. Stuck on a remote island with a man that should be in a museum for ladies' fantasies.

Yes, Holly Island is very much living up to expectations and this is one dream I don't ever want to wake up from.

CHAPTER 3

The warmth from the fire starts to thaw my frozen skin and gradually the feeling starts to return to my extremities. Curled up in the oversized chair, I think about my current situation. This is just my luck. The one time I throw caution to the wind and do something with my life, it backfires on me in a karma filled grenade.

This is my punishment for leaving Mr Saracen in the lurch at Christmas. God is punishing me for shattering Gregory's dreams of a happy ever after and mocking me for daring to think I could live on the edge.

I look up as the door opens and try to ignore the way my heart starts racing as I drool over the sight before me.

The man that even my dreams thought I didn't deserve is holding a mug of something with steam escaping and a plate of biscuits that looks as if they're homemade. I wonder if he quickly rustled them up earlier, reinforcing his god-like status and I smile gratefully as he hands me the mug and places the biscuits on the table between us. "Here, we may as well drink as many hot liquids as possible to stay warm. You look as if you could use something hot inside you, so don't hold back."

I almost pass out as my imagination takes a very explicit turn for the worse. Lifting the mug to my lips, I enjoy the warmth the steam offers my face as I take a sip of the sweet tea on offer.

I feel him watching me as he says, "We may as well introduce ourselves. My name's Leo and you are...?"

"Scarlett."

I smile shyly and he nods. "Well, Scarlett, I'm sorry to be the bearer of bad news but it looks as if you're stuck with me until we can work out what's happened."

I smile nervously and grip the mug just a little tighter as an awkward silence surrounds us. Leo leans back in his chair and stares at me gloomily and I can't think of a single intelligent thing to say to him because it appears that I've lost the art of conversation since I met him.

After a while, he sighs and shakes his head. "Listen, there's nothing we can do until the light returns, either by power or daylight. I'll grab us each a duvet and we can sleep here and consider our options in the morning."

He turns away and then, almost as an afterthought, says, "Are you hungry?"

I'm surprised to find that I am and say shyly, "Yes, a little, but I'll be fine with the biscuits."

He walks towards the door. "It's ok, I'll head to the kitchen and see if I can grab a few things. Stay here and keep warm. It's like a freezer out there and there's no sense in us both braving it."

As soon as he leaves, I quickly jump up and race across to the mirror above the fireplace and almost cry with frustration at the mess that looks back at me. My eyes are bloodshot and weary. The tangled mass on top of my head reminds me that I used to have hair, but it appears to have arranged itself into a very unflattering style, if you could even call it that. I have no make-up on, which is actually a blessing because it would surely be streaked all over my face and I'm so pale I could be mistaken for a ghost in this sure to be haunted mansion.

Quickly, I use my fingers to try to comb my hair into some sort of order and pinch my cheeks, briefly wondering if I should lean a little closer to the fire to scorch them into life. Deciding against it, I retreat quickly back to my chair when I hear footsteps in the hallway and try to look unconcerned as Leo strides into the room carrying a tray of sandwiches and what appear to be steaming bowls of soup. I say in surprise, "I thought you said we have no power."

Setting the tray down, he grins. "They have gas and I found the matches. At least we can heat things up on the stove, so it's not all bad news."

My heart dances what appears to be a samba inside me as I stare into the eyes of a man who could ruin women for a living. No, it's definitely not all bad and I smile as I take the warm bowl of soup gratefully and count my blessings. Yes, Holly Island is the place where dreams come true and I never want to leave.

ONCE WE HAVE EATEN, I start to feel a little sleepy. The fire has taken away the chill and the hot food has restored my body temperature enough that it now needs to rest and recharge what was used in getting here. The heat from the fire causes my eyelids to close and as I wrap the surrounding duvet a little tighter, I start to drift off to sleep.

Somehow, I manage to sleep sitting upright in a chair with a stranger seated just across from me. As I drift back to consciousness somewhere in the early hours, my limbs scream in protest as I gingerly uncurl my legs from under me and relish the blood returning to them. I blink as the light from the window dazzles me and reveals the secrets that the darkness obscured. The room is now different. Less cosy, less welcoming and much cooler. The morning light chases the shadows away and reveals an impressive room, decorated in blue and white with smart furnishings and tasteful ornaments. It appears to be clean and restores my faith a little as I see the evidence of a very smart hotel reveal itself after the harsh introduction last night.

Quickly, I look across at the empty chair and wonder if I dreamt of Leo. Maybe the darkness played tricks on me and an average man will walk into the room and laugh at my expense.

The clock on the wall chimes and I notice it's past 8 am and I feel myself relax. I'm here. It may not be what I expected, but that doesn't matter. I made the break, and this is the first morning of the rest of my life.

With newfound energy, I jump up and look around with happiness. This is an adventure, and it begins here and now.

Humming to myself, I venture out of the room, still wrapped in the blanket, and go in search of my companion. As I wander from room to room, my excitement increases with every step taken. This hotel is amazing and is everything I thought it was and more. It's cosy and comfortable yet filled with splendour. It's clean and inviting and I marvel at the gleaming surfaces and tastefully arranged flower arrangements on every surface.

I find myself in a room that must be used as a bar and look with delight at the sparkling decanters filled with amber liquid. I see rows of spirits hanging from the bar, below which are gleaming glasses lined up and waiting to be filled. It may be as cold as an igloo, but the warmth in my heart more than makes up for it. I love it here.

Suddenly, the door opens and brings inside an icy blast as Leo struggles in under the weight of some logs for the fire. Dumping them on the ground, he sighs heavily, "That should keep us going until lunchtime."

He looks up and I feel my heart lurch as I take in the man himself in daylight. He is every bit as impressive as I thought he was last night and if anything, the daylight just makes him look even better.

He smiles and nods towards a door at the end of the hall-way. "I don't know about you, but I'm starving. Why don't we grab some breakfast and then see about making the best of the situation?"

I nod and follow him through the impressive entrance hall towards a door at the end. This door leads to another passageway and we walk toward another door that, when opened, reveals a large industrial kitchen.

I look with wonder at the clean, stainless-steel world and imagine it bustling with staff and filled with amazing smells and activity.

Leo heads towards a large industrial fridge and says happily, "Eggs and bacon coming up."

He spins around and says quickly, "You're not a vegetarian, are you?"

"No, I'll eat anything."

He raises his eyes and I laugh. "It's true. To be honest, I'm one of those girls who can't say no."

He smirks and I say quickly, "To food, of course... um... yes... food. I'll try anything once. I've always have had the spirit of adventure running through my veins. Oh yes, that's me, a real girl guide and Dora the explorer, um... can I help with anything?"

I blush as I realise how much my babbling makes me look like an imbecile, and he shrugs. "You could find some bread. The power's not on yet but we could toast it on the fire."

Grateful for the distraction, I almost run to what I think is an enormous pantry in the corner of the room, while Leo sets about lighting the gas burners and filling the frying pans with eggs and bacon.

Soon the delicious scent of bacon frying fills the room and my mouth waters. I'm in heaven.

We work well together as we each perform our tasks quickly and in sync, and soon we have a feast laid out on the bench before us. Plates of eggs, bacon and fried bread and tomatoes sit steaming before us. Freshly squeezed orange juice sits in crystal tumblers, and large slices of crusty bread await the toasting fork as we carry our feast towards the small room we now call home.

As we set the food down on the table, Leo spies a toasting fork in the cluster of fire utensils and pounces on it eagerly. "Great, I've always wanted to do this. Throw me a slice of bread and I'll toast it for you."

I do as I'm told and watch as he holds it to the fire and says quickly, "Eat up before it gets cold. This won't take long."

I need no further invitation and start tucking in, savouring the delicious taste of a breakfast fit for a king. Leo hands me the toasted bread and I smear liberal amounts of butter and marmalade on it and relish the hot, sweet taste that explodes on my tongue. Leo settles down opposite me and wolfs his down and I try to stop myself from groaning out loud as I savour every minute of this amazing breakfast.

He looks at me with curiosity and says, "So, what brings you here, don't you have anyone to share Christmas with?"

His words bring me back to reality and I stare back at him miserably. "I'm running away from it all, if you must know. I needed some time on my own to re-evaluate my life and needed space to do it."

"Why?"

"Because I'm stuck in a rut and the only way out is marriage to a man, I don't love. Don't get me wrong, I do love him in a fond way, but not as I imagined love would be. More like friends really."

I swallow hard as his eyes penetrate mine and he says in a husky voice, "So, what's missing?"

I shrug and try to tear my gaze away. "Excitement, I suppose. I do enjoy Gregory's company. It's just that it's not like the books I read. He doesn't set my pulse racing and my toes tingling."

I feel embarrassed as he laughs softly and I blush. "Ok, bad choice of words. The thing is, Leo, how do you know when you've met the one? Maybe Gregory is my one and I'm blinded by the stories I read."

"So, you read romance."

I stare at him in surprise. "Of course. I work in a book-shop and think I've read most of them. It's a good place to dream and maybe that's the problem. My expectations have been raised so high they're impossible to reach."

Leo nods and carries on eating and I say with interest, "Your turn, same question."

"Same answer."

I stare at him in surprise as he sighs. "I'm also running away. I'm expected to marry a girl I don't love and pursue a career I hate."

I feel intrigued and lean forward eagerly. "What career?"

"Banking. Ever since I graduated from Uni, I've been tied to a desk at my uncle's company. I'm expected to rise through the ranks and join him on the board one day. The thing is, I hate it. It's suffocating me and dragging me down and is the last thing I want to do with my life."

"What do you want to do?"

I think I hold my breath as his eyes sparkle and he looks

animated. "Write. I'm an author in my spare time and I would love nothing more than to make it full time."

I stare at him in surprise. "What do you write?"

"Stories."

He stands and gathers the empty plates onto the tray, signifying the end of the conversation. I can tell he doesn't want me to pry, and I respect his privacy. As I follow him to the kitchen, I think about Leo. I would never have guessed he's an author. He looks like a Hollywood star, and I can see why banking stifles him. I think about the woman he's marrying and feel jealous, although I have no reason to. As I follow him, I say loudly, "What about your fiancée? Does she know you're here?"

"No. I left without telling her. Not that she'll even notice I've gone until she needs me to accompany her to some boring event. You see, unlike me, Davina is a social climber and is all about appearances and connections. We're actually poles apart and she would absolutely hate it here. Last night would have sent her over the edge and that's why I know I've done the right thing. Distance can solve many a problem and clear the way. I'm not going back to that life and, when I leave this place, it will be on my own terms; if we ever get the chance to leave, that is."

"What do you mean?"

His words set off the warning sirens, and he shakes his head. "The only way back is by boat and there is no way of calling one to rescue us."

"That's crazy, we just need to phone for one."

Leo laughs. "If only it were that easy. You know the old sailor that brought us here?"

"Yes."

"Well, I asked him for his number should I need a lift and he told me he only did arrivals."

"Arrivals?"

"Yes. Apparently, he doesn't do departures because that's his brother's job. When I asked for his number, he told me he didn't have one. So, I asked how we arrange to leave and he told me that it's all worked into our booking. On our last day, his brother turns up and takes us home. In the meantime, we're on our own."

"That's ridiculous."

I roll my eyes and laugh. "We just need to google another boat; it can't be that difficult."

Leo shakes his head. "You'd think so, wouldn't you? The trouble is, they are the only boats here and unless you're a strong swimmer, I doubt we're leaving anytime soon."

We start to wash up the breakfast things and I congratulate myself on how things are working out. Stranded on a remote island with a man who makes all others look like boys. This place really is the stuff of dreams because I now have two weeks with this man spent in a well-stocked hotel with no other guests. I must have done something right in my life to deserve such a reward. He can't get away and is now completely at my mercy. What could go wrong?

CHAPTER 4

*a*fter breakfast, Leo turns to me and says lightly, "Maybe you should grab a bedroom that you like the look of and unpack. I'll try to see if there's a way of getting power and then maybe we can start to enjoy the break we paid for."

He heads off, and I set about exploring the place I'll call home for the next two weeks. Once I've retrieved my suitcase, I head towards a large staircase that dominates the hallway. I feel like Scarlett O'Hara as I pass the impressive paintings and tread on deep pile carpet held down by stair rods. I feel a tingle of excitement as I wonder what lies behind every door I come to. Each room is special for a different reason. They all appear to be themed, and where some are modern, others are traditional. There are four-poster beds and in one there's even a water bed. Some rooms are single with an ensuite, whereas others are suites made up of a couple of rooms with settees and tables and balconies that reveal breath-taking views.

There's not one room I don't love and I find it hard to choose. Finally, I settle on a room that overlooks the water's edge. The décor is light and airy and the yellow wallpaper brings the sunshine in. The bed is warm and cosy and much larger than my one at home.

As I unpack my things I feel at peace with my decision. The birds sing outside my window and even the sun makes a welcome appearance. The storm appears to be behind us and I feel positive about the weeks ahead.

As I stare out onto the landscape, I notice a boat on the water fast approaching. Squinting, I can just make out it's the same one that brought me here and my heart starts thumping. Quickly, I spin on my heels and race to the door calling out as I go, "Leo, quickly, someone's coming."

As I tear down the stairs, Leo appears from a room further down the hall and says, "What is it?"

"The boat's coming and there are people on board. It may be the staff."

Grabbing our coats, we head out of the door and start running down the path without stopping to question why. Maybe it's because it's the first thing that's happened and we need answers but I soon find myself panting as I struggle to keep up. Halfway down the path, Leo turns around and reaching out, grabs my hand and pulls me behind him. I don't even have time to enjoy the feeling of his hand in mine as we reach the jetty just as the boat pulls up alongside.

"Ahoy there me hearties."

I stifle a grin as Leo looks in bewilderment at the rather smart elderly gentleman sitting proudly in the boat with his back straight and a superior look on his face. The lady that accompanies him is an elegant woman who is wearing a rather impressive fur coat with a sailor hat. She waves excitedly as the boat pulls alongside the jetty and Leo offers his hand to the elderly gentleman. "Yoo-hoo, permission to come ashore."

She giggles as the man leaps from the boat with a youthfulness that belies his appearance and turns to offer her his hand. "My lady."

She giggles and stumbles out of the boat and looks around her with excitement. "Lovely, darling. This is just lovely."

The man looks across at Leo and says stiffly, "Would you be so kind as to take our luggage to your best room?"

Leo looks a little shocked and I say quickly, "I'm sorry, we don't work here, we're guests too."

The man looks shocked. "Good god man, please accept my apologies. Where are the porters around here?"

Leo smiles. "There aren't any but I would be happy to help."

Reaching inside the boat, he hauls their cases from inside with ease and the woman looks at him wistfully and then turns to me and winks. "Lovely, darling. You're very lucky."

I feel my cheeks flame as I stutter, "Oh no, we're not um… together or anything."

Leo grins as the woman shakes her head. "Never mind darling, maybe Santa will do the honours."

I'm grateful when Leo says loudly, "Excuse me, please can you tell us what happened to the staff?"

The Hagrid lookalike shakes his head as he starts pulling away from the jetty. "Can't help you, I only deal with arrivals."

Leo shouts, "Who will know?"

"My brother, he deals with departures."

"Could you ask him and let us know?" I shout desperately as he pulls even further away.

Hagrid shakes his head. "No."

The engine cuts in and drowns out any further conversation and Leo groans with exasperation. "For god's sake, what is this place?"

The couple looks bemused and I hold out my hand. "I'm

sorry, I'm Scarlett and this is Leo. We're guests too but there appears to be no staff."

They look amazed, and the woman says, "Whatever next. I'm Alice and this fine specimen is Harold. He's an ex-Navy captain you know."

She beams with pride as Harold holds out his hand and shakes mine vigorously. "Pleased to meet you, young lady."

He looks across at Leo and booms, "Do you need a hand with that luggage, son?"

Before Leo can answer he says loudly, "Ok, thanks."

He turns to Alice and takes her arm. "Come my darling, let's find us the best room and rest our weary heads for a while before lunch."

I watch in bewilderment as they head off down the path without a backward glance and stare at Leo in surprise. "What just happened?"

Laughing, he hoists the two immense suitcases, one under each arm and grins, "It's fine. At least we have company I suppose."

We follow behind the elderly couple and I whisper, "I wonder what will happen? I mean, I can't see them making their own breakfast and stuff. This could all go badly wrong."

"Well, I'm not waiting on them. I'm here to finish the book I'm writing. I'll muck in when I need to but that's all."

As we follow them towards the hotel, I try to reassure myself that it's not so bad. We'll all be fine. I'm sure we can pull together and the staff may be back before the day ends, anyway.

However, I remain unconvinced as we head back along the dusty path because there's something telling me that things can only get worse.

CHAPTER 5

*B*y the time Harold and Alice find a room they like an hour has gone by. They decide on one of the more superior suites and then inform us they will be taking a siesta and don't want to be disturbed. I try to shut out the shrieks as the door closes and banish the images that are now firmly planted in my mind as we leave them to it.

Leo grins as we head downstairs. "Lively, aren't they?"

"Yes, they are a bit. I wonder what they'll make of life in a deserted hotel."

We hear the sound of laughter following us and Leo says quickly, "Fancy a walk?"

Nodding gratefully, I follow him outside, making sure to grab a nearby blanket to help beat off the cold.

We head the other way towards the impressive gardens that surround the hotel, and I look around with interest.

"This place is beautiful."

As I look, the view takes my breath away. The landscape is obviously very well maintained because there is not a blade of grass out of place. Festive shrubs are in full bloom and the evergreen trees stand like proud soldiers guarding the crown jewels. The eye is drawn beyond the garden to view the glittering sea in the distance and even the birds are singing after the severe storm has passed. I can't help but raise a smile at the sheer beauty of it all, and as I turn to Leo, he laughs. "You're easily impressed."

"How can you say that? This place is beautiful. I have never seen such a view. Don't you agree?"

"Maybe, but it doesn't really compare to some of the places I have visited."

Turning away, I decide that Leo may be amazing looking, but there's a side to him that I don't care for. However, nothing is going to spoil this moment for me because, unlike him, I have never seen such a view in my life.

I can feel him studying me and feel a little irritated. He's ruining this moment for me when I am at one with nature and detoxing my mind. I move away and try to take a few cleansing breaths of sea air to restore my inner calm, but the moment is ruined again when he complains, "I'm freezing, maybe we should get a move on."

Spinning around, I say irritably, "Then go back inside. I'm fine on my own. Maybe you should return to the hotel and finish your book."

He looks a little surprised at the curt way I spoke to him. "Is that what you want?"

I nod. "Yes, I could do with some alone time, if you don't mind."

He makes to speak and then must think better of it because he smiles and turns to head back the way we came.

The wind blows and I pull my blanket around me a little tighter and curse the moment my dream man turned into Mr Average. Why couldn't we be kindred spirits who marvelled at the beauty of nature in one shared voice? Why couldn't he declare his undying love for me minutes after we met, after discovering we are soul mates? Then again, why am I such an idiot and look for the impossible in reality? Maybe I have been stuck in that bookshop with my head in fiction for far too long. Prince Charming always was a mythical creature, anyway. Perhaps there is no such thing as perfection and I should stop looking for it.

Thinking of Gregory worrying back at home, I feel a sudden pang. Gregory would love this view. He would be interested in the various plant species and take photographs to catalogue in his memory box. He would insist that we explore every inch of this horticultural paradise and then spend the evening swatting up on the things we found and learning everything about them. Gregory wouldn't have dismissed the view so airily or complained of the cold. Then again, Gregory wouldn't make my heart race even a tiny bit as fast as it races when Leo regards me with those chocolate velvet eyes. Gregory wouldn't make me long for just a smile from his heavenly lips or melt as he holds my hand. Is it possible that somewhere there's a 'Greo' for me - the best of both and my dream man?

Shivering, as another icy blast reminds me why it's not a good idea to stop for too long near water in Winter, I start walking towards the sea. I stamp my feet to restore the circulation and try to piece together what it is I actually want.

As I near the shore, I notice what appears to be a ramshackle boathouse nestling by the water's edge. As I draw near, I make out the weathered wood that is splintered and decaying, held together by a rope. The little jetty that leads off from it appears to be missing vital pieces and yet I catch sight of a flash of white and edge further forward, my curiosity pushing my caution aside.

As I clamber down the bank towards the ramshackle building, I feel like an explorer. There is something inside this crumbling wreck of a boathouse and I mean to find out what.

Carefully, I navigate the pieces of junk that litter the bank and draw near the entrance. The cold no longer bothers me as the adrenalin kicks in and before long, I reach my prize.

Tethered to a ring on the jetty is a little speedboat. It looks in good condition and I smile at the engine sitting proudly on the back of the boat and marvel at the gleaming white fibreglass that looks almost brand new.

My heart lifts as I realise we have a way off this Island should we need it. So much for Hagrid and his brother, we are self-sufficient and can make our own choices. This is a fantastic find.

The fact that I don't know the first thing about starting it, let alone driving it, doesn't even cross my mind. I can google that and then I'll be an expert.

Then I think about it and wonder what I'm thinking. I've just got here. Why on earth would I want to leave?

I feel a few spots of rain hit me and look up at the sudden cluster of angry-looking clouds. From out of nowhere, a storm is gathering and I probably don't have long before the heavens will open.

Quickly, I start to make my way up the bank, but I'm not prepared for how slippery it is. As I slip back down, I catch my foot in a coil of old rope and fall back, twisting my ankle as I go. The pain is sharp and brings tears to my eyes as the rain starts lashing down mercilessly.

I try to claw my way up the bank but my gloves allow me no grip, so in exasperation I rip them off and grip the wet grass with my fingers as I try to haul myself up.

My breathing is ragged as the pain consumes me and I start to sob with frustration because I am helpless in the face of adversity and my special moment is turning into a bad memory.

Suddenly, I hear a shout and my heart lifts. It must be Leo, thank God.

However, a different face appears over the horizon and I look with surprise at the man who is charging towards me. From a distance, he looks not much older than me and I wonder if more visitors have arrived. I wince with pain as my ankle throbs and as he draws near, I gasp, "I think I've twisted my ankle."

I watch as he throws a rope towards me and cries, "Grip the rope and I'll haul you up the bank."

Like a cowboy lassoing a horse, he throws me the rope and I grasp it eagerly. Then, with just a few hefty pulls, I feel myself being pulled up the slippery bank and into the arms of a very capable rescuer.

He looks at me with concern and then grins lopsidedly and winks. "Come on, I'll get you to safety."

I'm surprised when, in one swift move, he swings me into his arms and carries me effortlessly through the trees. Even my throbbing ankle can't ruin what is turning into one of the happiest moments of my life. This is unreal. A fantasy come true and worthy of inclusion in any Jane Austen novel. This is my Mr Darcy and as I snuggle into the strong chest of the man holding me so carefully, I thank God and Facebook I saw the ad for Holly Island.

CHAPTER 6

To my surprise, my rescuer heads away from the hotel and I wonder where he's taking me. I don't even question his motives because I am so swept up in the sheer romance of the situation. The wind blows around us fiercely and the rain lashes down, cancelling out any conversation and I just savour the moment for what it's worth.

As we turn a corner, I am surprised to see a lovely little cottage nestling in a sheltered spot and can smell wood smoke billowing from a chimney.

The little garden that surrounds the cottage looks well maintained, and I look with interest at a gleaming red door with a polished letterbox. My rescuer kicks open the door and we stumble into a warm, cosy entrance and the smell of baking greets me making my mouth water. This place must surely be paradise.

As he sets me down, a woman appears dusting the flour off her hands and says with surprise, "What happened?"

"Found her by the boathouse. I think she's sprained her ankle."

The woman makes a clucking noise and says quickly, "Help her to the settee and I'll take a look."

Finding this all a little strange, I say nervously, "Um… I'm sorry to trouble you."

The woman smiles warmly. "You're not. Let me introduce us. I'm Marigold Hinchley and this is my son Ryan."

"Oh, I'm pleased to meet you. I'm Scarlett Robins, a guest at the hotel."

I watch them share a look and the woman sighs. "Oh dear."

Ryan takes my arm and says kindly, "Here, let me help you."

I follow him into a small cosy living room where the fire roars in an inglenook fireplace. The light is dim, lit only by a solitary candle, but the welcome is warm as he settles me into a comfortable chair and says with interest, "You must be one of the guests who never got the email."

"Email?"

Marigold nods. "Yes, terrible business really."

Ryan nods. "Yes, totally unexpected."

He looks at his mother and shakes his head. "Maybe you should fetch Scarlett some tea while I take a look at her ankle."

Marigold rolls her eyes, "Of course, where are my manners? I won't be long; you're in safe hands."

She winks as she leaves the room, and Ryan laughs softly. "Don't mind her, Scarlett. She'll talk about this for months. She doesn't get much excitement these days, so you have done me a great service in potentially injuring your ankle and allowing me to rescue you from an almost certain death."

He laughs as he crouches before me and gently lifts my injured ankle.

I wince as he starts to remove my boot, and he smiles

apologetically. "Sorry, I need to assess the damage, I'll be as careful as possible."

I feel a little self-conscious as he contemplates my ankle that feels as if it's on fire. "Um… I'm sorry to be so much trouble. You've been very kind."

"It's nothing. You know, you have nothing to worry about. I am sort of trained in medicine."

"Sort of?"

"Yes, I've just qualified as a vet."

He laughs as I raise my eyes and giggle. "Well, that's a relief. I mean, I'm sure you must have dealt with many an animal's ankle injury."

He laughs and I wince as he presses on a particularly tender spot and he shakes his head. "I think it's just a gentle sprain. A little rest and you'll be as good as new in no time."

Marigold heads back into the room and my mouth waters as I see three steaming mugs of what smells like hot chocolate and some amazing looking chocolate muffins beside them.

"Here you go, Scarlett, get this down you and you'll feel as right as rain."

Gratefully, I take a warm mug of heaven and laugh. "There's nothing right about rain today. That came out of the blue."

She laughs. "It does that here. One minute the sun is shining, and all is right with the world, the next the heavens open and the place resembles a scene from the Titanic. It plays havoc with my washing, you know."

Ryan catches my eye and grins and I smile back, feeling warm for a different reason this time because Ryan is seriously cute. Blond hair, slightly spiky on top, frames an angelic face. Two of the bluest eyes I have ever seen sparkle and the strong hands that grip me cause a shiver that no amount of rain and wind could match. He looks to be a similar age to me, and I can't help but feel a surge of interest for my intrepid hero.

They settle down in the seat opposite and Marigold says with a slight edge to her voice, "Shocking business."

"What, the hotel?" I say with interest while savouring the sweetest tasting hot chocolate.

She nods and her lips purse together in a thin line. "I can't believe the Scotts just upped and went with no regard for the bookings. Most unprofessional if you ask me."

"What happened to make them leave?"

I can tell that Marigold is itching to divulge the information due to the excitement that sparks in her eyes and she lowers her voice as if there are hidden interested parties. "The Scott family ran Holly Island hotel. In fact, they have done for close on twenty years and made it into the business it is today. It was their baby, and they took great pride in it."

Ryan nods and Marigold sighs heavily. "They didn't own it though and the people that did sold it to a developer for rather a lot of money and they were given notice to leave along with the rest of the staff. As soon as Christmas was over, they would be out of a job, so you can imagine the shock they all felt."

I feel horrified and picture the devastation the announcement must have caused.

Marigold continues breathlessly. "Well, they were angry and told the staff they may as well head home for Christmas because why bother to stay and line the pockets of the very people who sold them out? The Scotts booked a cruise to the Caribbean and left the very next week. They told me they had cancelled the bookings by email, but I'm guessing they didn't catch them all. So, now you're all turning up and there's no staff to deliver the promise of a happy Christmas. Shameful if you ask me."

I stare at her in shock, and Ryan nods. "Yes, it's a shame innocent people have been caught up in this whole fiasco."

He looks across at me as he places his arm around his mother's shoulders and says sadly, "Mum was one of the staff who lost her job. She was the housekeeper, in charge of maintaining the rooms. Now she has no job and no income."

Marigold sighs. "I'm not sure what to do really because this cottage came with the job. I'm guessing I'll have to vacate it in the new year to make way for the developers."

I feel bad for her and say gently, "Is there anything you can do?"

"Not really." She says sadly. "I've applied for a couple of housekeeper positions on the mainland, but it's Christmas, so nobody's doing much this side of the new year. It will be an uncertain few weeks while my predicament is put on hold for the festivities."

Ryan squeezes her shoulder and says gently, "You know I'll look after you, don't you mum?"

She smiles sweetly and my eyes fill with tears. This is heart-breaking. They are so sweet together and seeing the genuine love they have for one another is making my heart ache. Suddenly, Marigold laughs loudly. "Anyway, enough of all this doom and gloom. It doesn't help anything and I intend to make the most of my last Christmas on Holly Island. I've got food in the cupboard and logs for the fire. My son has returned to make it a special occasion and I can look forward to a fresh start in the new year somewhere amazing."

I catch Ryan's eye and smile sympathetically, but don't miss the worry in his eyes.

As I take a sip of the heavenly chocolate, Marigold says eagerly, "You know, maybe we could all pull together and make this Christmas count. I'm guessing the other guests won't mind if we organise something. After all, they've been promised a Christmas to remember. Just because it's not quite what they thought it would be, we could still make it special."

I suppose I'm caught up in the whole crazy situation because I say eagerly, "Oh yes, we must. Count me in. What do you have in mind?"

Ryan shakes his head and holds up his hand. "Whoa, wait a minute. Scarlett, you are one of the guests. You shouldn't have to do anything and mum, I don't think even you can do everything."

Marigold looks at him crossly. "I'll do what I want, Ryan. You should know that more than most. No, if Scarlett wants to help out, she's more than welcome. It's not as if I'm intending on doing everything, anyway. No, all I want is to send Holly Island hotel out in style and give it the Christmas it deserves with the few special people who are staying here."

Ryan smiles sweetly, "Then you have my full support."

Marigold looks quite emotional, so I cough discreetly and say brightly, "I should be getting back. If you could point me in the right direction, I'd be most grateful."

Ryan stands and holds out his hand. "I'll walk you back and if need be, I can give you a piggyback."

As I gingerly test out my ankle, he offers his support and I say gratefully, "Thank you, both of you. I meant what I said. I'll only be too happy to help out with making Christmas a good one for everyone. Just let me know what you need me to do."

Marigold smiles and I see the excitement causing her eyes to sparkle. "Don't you worry, Scarlett, this will be the best Christmas of your life. You just wait and see."

CHAPTER 7

I don't even notice the chill in the air as we walk back to the hotel. I don't notice that my ankle is throbbing and I appear to have developed a limp. All I can think of is how lovely Ryan and Marigold are, and I must help them.

As we walk, I say thoughtfully, "What do you think your mother will do?"

"I'm not sure." He sighs sadly. "Ever since my father died, I've been worried about her."

"Oh, I'm sorry."

He shrugs. "You weren't to know. They both worked here, and he was the handyman. He repaired things, helped the gardeners, chopped the logs and between them they kept the place running. Then last year he fell ill and ended up in a hospice within a few weeks. At least it was quick, but mum was lost for a while without him."

I feel sad at his words and say, "I'm sorry, it must have been a difficult time."

"It was - still is actually and now this has happened. It's the icing on the cake. You see, Holly Island is mum's home as well as her place of work. She's getting close to retirement and I'm not so sure she'll find it easy to find another position."

We see the hotel lights before us and he laughs softly. "It looks as if the power came back on. That's good, at least you should be more comfortable as a result."

I look up in surprise because, quite frankly, I had forgotten about that. "Goodness, for a moment there it slipped my mind. Your mum must have had another source of power because those cakes were still warm."

"She has an Aga. Nothing stops that beast. It's essential on Holly Island to have every kind of power source available. They're quite unreliable and you should always have a backup."

As we near the hotel, I hear a voice calling me, "Scarlett, are you there?"

Recognising Leo's voice, I shout, "Over here."

Ryan looks at the figure racing towards us and says with interest, "Is that your boyfriend?"

Laughing, I shake my head. "No, another guest. He must have wondered where I got to."

It doesn't take him long and Leo reaches us completely out of breath and looking soaked to the skin. He stares at Ryan in surprise and I'm shocked to see how anxious he looks as he says quickly, "Oh, thank God, I've been worried sick. The storm blew up out of nowhere and I came to find you, but you appeared to have disappeared without a trace. Are you ok?"

He looks at Ryan and appears a little guarded as he holds out his hand. "Hi, I'm Ryan. I found Scarlett in the boathouse. I think she's twisted her ankle but with a bit of rest she should be ok."

I'm surprised to see the concern in Leo's eyes as he looks

at me with a worried expression. "Is that right Scarlett? Can I get you anything?"

Laughing, I roll my eyes. "Only a nice seat by that fire you make so well. I think I've had more than enough excitement for one day."

Ryan laughs. "I'll leave you in what I can see are capable hands. It was a pleasure, Scarlett, and no doubt our paths will cross again tomorrow."

We grin at each other and I say gratefully, "Thanks. I really appreciate what you did and will look forward to discussing things further."

Ryan nods and with a brief smile, turns and heads back to the cottage.

Leo looks concerned. "Let me help you inside. I feel so bad for deserting you and now this has happened."

I take his arm gratefully and shake my head. "It's not your fault. I was an idiot. I should never have told you to leave me alone. It was rude and I apologise."

We walk back and Leo says softly, "You were right to say it, though. I behaved like an ass. I suppose I'm so used to looking without seeing, I've forgotten how to appreciate the finer things in life."

"Finer things?"

He nods. "Yes, the finer things, and I'm not talking about the material ones either. You were right, it is an amazing view. In fact, it's an amazing place and I should never have taken it for granted. You see, I am so used to doing everything at a million miles an hour, I don't stop to look sometimes. For example, a sunset or the sound of waves crashing to the shore is much better than watching a good drama on the television or having a nice meal. Sometimes we forget the riches that go unmentioned every day and just take them for granted. You were right to give me the cold shoulder, so don't apologise."

Silence falls between us as I struggle to take in his words. I can't believe it, Leo just apologised for something that was so meaningless in the grand scheme of it all. I feel a little bad and say warmly. "No, I apologise. It wasn't my place to pass comment. Let's just forget about it and carry on with our day."

We are almost to the front entrance and Leo laughs. "I think Harold and Alice have made themselves at home. When I left, they were drinking the bar dry. They were quite excited at the fact there was nobody to curb their intake, so I'm not sure what we'll find when we get inside."

As we stumble through the door, I hear loud shrieks accompanied by much deeper ones and grin. "I dread to think what's going on in there."

Leo pulls me towards the little snug room that seems almost like home and says firmly, "You go and relax and I'll rustle us all up some food. I think they could use it and I don't know about you but I'm starving."

I watch him head off and limp towards my comfy chair by the fire. As I watch the flames dance a merry dance before me, I feel happy inside. What a day this is turning out to be and now things are looking brighter. The power is restored and we have company. Ryan and Marigold could well become good friends and I am looking forward to spending a lovely Christmas with all of them.

CHAPTER 8

*T*he next day dawns and as the sunlight streams through a crack in the curtains, I relish the warm cosy feeling that's a result of a good night's sleep. Leo managed to rustle up some pain killers, enabling me to have a relatively pain-free night, and even Harold and Alice quietened down and lent a hand with the washing up.

As I think about my fellow guests, I laugh to myself. What an odd bunch we are. I wonder if any more guests will show up, in a way I hope not because, with Ryan and Marigold and their Christmas extravaganza I've volunteered to help with, this trip is looking very promising indeed.

Now I've unpacked, I feel more at home than ever. The power is back on and I treat myself to a long, hot shower. I start to feel more like myself and dress in some warm leggings and a thick sweater and head downstairs in search of food.

The place appears deserted, so I head to the kitchen to see if I can start breakfast. However, as soon as I push the door open, a mouth-watering aroma greets me as I detect bacon frying and coffee brewing. I'm surprised to see Marigold working away, and she looks up and grins. "Morning Scarlett, I hope you slept well."

"Yes, thank you, but why are you working, Marigold? You should be taking it easy now."

She shrugs. "I may as well do what I love and spend the next few weeks of my time on Holly Island doing what I do best. It struck me last night that I was being selfish and depriving myself of enjoyment."

"You call this enjoyment?" I smile and she laughs softly. "Actually, yes. I definitely class this as enjoying myself. I always have loved cooking and caring for people. Now I can please myself without having strict menus to follow and timesheets to fill in. I was never allowed to cook because the chef was very protective of his kitchen and would be horrified to allow a mere cook inside. I'm loving picturing his face as I do everything he would hate; it's quite invigorating."

I smile and feel glad that she's happy. "Well, let me do something to help. I'll lay the table in the dining room and act as your waitress. It will be fun."

We busy ourselves making breakfast and I find that I'm really enjoying myself. Marigold is good company and an easy companion. It doesn't take long and we soon have a meal prepared that the absent chef would certainly approve of, so I head out to see if I can rustle up some guests to make it all worthwhile.

As I climb the impressive staircase, I marvel at how this trip has turned out. I never thought it would end up like this and I wonder if I would be as happy if the staff had stayed.

I knock on Harold and Alice's door and shout, "Breakfast is ready in the dining room if you want some."

Then I head along the hall to what I think must be Leo's room. I saw him coming out of a door a few doors away from mine yesterday and hope this is the right one. I knock tentatively. "Leo, breakfast is ready when you are."

There's no answer, so he's either still sleeping or has gone for an early morning walk.

I head back downstairs and meet Marigold in the dining room, and she smiles warmly. "Right, it's all warming on the side and I have filled the coffee and teapots. You should have everything you need so I'll leave you to it and head back to clear up and start preparing lunch."

As she turns to leave, I say quickly, "Wait, aren't you going to join us?"

"Goodness me, no. I ate hours ago. I'm happier just pottering around doing my own thing. Don't worry about me, I'm more than happy playing at this."

She heads off and I look at the feast she's prepared. It looks mouth-watering and I soon tuck into a plate of eggs, bacon, and tomato with toast and marmalade. I feel a little put out that nobody bothered to show after all the hard work she's put into it and feel a little lonely as I eat on my own surrounded by empty seats.

As I sip my third cup of tea, the door opens and Alice heads inside looking as if she's royalty in a silk dress and pearls, with her hair neatly curled and her lips painted red.

"Morning Scarlett and what an amazing one it is."

"Morning Alice, did you sleep well?"

"Not much sleep went on, if you know what I mean?"

She winks and I stifle a grin as she grabs a bowl of yoghurt and helps herself to some fruit.

"You know, I may need a little forty winks after breakfast because Harold has drained me of any energy I had, not that I have a lot of it these days."

She giggles as she peels her apple and says wistfully, "You know, I never thought I'd be this happy at my time of life."

I lean forward and smile. "Why do you say that?"

"When my beloved Fred died, I was a lost woman. It took me a while to come to terms with it, and I wasn't sure which direction to take. I suppose I withdrew into myself but then a couple of weeks later I spied an advert in the local library."

"Two weeks?" I say faintly.

She nods sadly. "Yes, that's two weeks. I'll never get back. Anyway, I saw an advert for the Holmbury over 60s dating service and thought I'd give it a go."

She smiles wistfully and looks as if she's lost in happy memories. "You would never believe how many men and women I may add, I meet at our weekly get-togethers. I've had many pleasurable trips with other like-minded people and seen some amazing places. You know, when Harold mentioned this place, I was the first to jump at the chance."

"The first?" My head starts spinning as I imagine the whole of the Holmbury dating club descending on Holly Island.

She laughs. "Yes, Mavis Williams looked green with envy when I pipped her to the post. Harold is considered quite a catch in the club and it pays to be quick off the blocks."

My head spins as I struggle to keep up and say in confusion, "I'm sorry, Alice, I thought Harold was your husband."

She laughs loudly and shakes her head. "Good god no. Why would I want one man when there are so many on offer. You know, I was married for forty-two years to Fred and I don't think we had as much sex in the whole of it as I've had since joining the club. It's a whole new world out there and I'm grabbing it with both hands."

She looks at me sympathetically. "Don't settle for one man when there are so many out there. If you meet a rich one, though, hold on to him because they're in short supply. No, I may be spending Christmas with Harold, but I'm spending New Year in the Swiss Alps with Bert Cartwright. It's all arranged, you know, unless his heart gives out after a stint with Elsie Jones in the Lake District. From what I've heard, she's a wild one."

The door opens, saving me from responding, and Harold enters the room looking bleary-eyed and exhausted. His eyes light up when he sees Alice though, and he plants a sweet kiss on her lips before turning to me and saying loudly, "Morning my dear, you're looking delightful, may I say."

I feel myself getting a little hot as I see the look they share and say quickly, "Thank you. Anyway, I should be heading out for some fresh air. Enjoy your breakfast."

I think I escape the room in a world record as I charge outside in desperate need of normality. Whatever next?

CHAPTER 9

*J*t's only as I venture outside that my ankle reminds me it's not willing to accompany me and I feel exasperated that I'll have to forego a brisk walk along the shoreline.

As I head inside, I wonder whether to help Marigold with the dishes, but then I see Leo heading my way looking a little distracted.

He looks up and smiles wearily before lowering his voice. "Morning Scarlett, how's your ankle?"

"Fine thanks. There's some breakfast in the dining room courtesy of our new staff member."

"Staff member?"

I smile. "I'll fill you in after you've eaten. Word of warning though, Alice and Harold are in there and you may not be prepared for their conversation."

I laugh to myself at his confused expression as I head off to explore a little more of this lovely hotel. I may not be up to walking far, but I can hobble around the immaculate hallways and delve into the secrets of this place.

I feel like an intruder as I make my way into dozens of

rooms, marvelling at the luxurious furnishings and amazing views from the windows.

By the time Leo finds me about an hour later, I have found the library and am tucked up on a window seat with Wuthering Heights, as I look out across the dramatic landscape.

He heads towards me and raises his eyes. "I didn't have you down as a classics lover."

"Why, what did you have me down as?"

He takes the seat opposite and smiles. "You told me you liked romance. I suppose I thought you read Mills and Boon or that sort of thing."

"Maybe I do. It doesn't stop me from enjoying other types, though. What about you, you said you write stories, let me guess, thrillers or mysteries perhaps?"

Suddenly, the shutters come down and he says quickly, "Something like that. Anyway, tell me what happened yesterday."

As I fill him in, it strikes me that whatever Leo writes is strictly private. I'm even more interested now because it's obvious he's not keen to divulge any information about his own books, which makes me wonder why. By the time I finish my story, he looks amazed. "I can't believe they sold this place. I wonder what it will be?"

"I don't know. I hope it stays as a hotel, though. It's such a magical place it would be a shame to close it off from the world."

He looks thoughtful. "I wonder how we can find out."

I say in surprise. "Why would you be interested? I mean, I'm sure after Christmas you'll return home and not give this place another thought."

"Maybe, maybe not." He leans forward. "You know, Scarlett, I think you have quite a low opinion of me."

I blush and say quickly, "Why do you say that?"

"Because you are so quick to judge based on a few words spoken. Maybe you should get to know someone before forming your opinion on them."

I don't get to answer him because suddenly all hell breaks loose as we hear loud voices calling, "Is anybody there, for God's sake, call this a hotel?"

Leo looks at me in surprise and I groan. "It sounds as if there are a few new arrivals. Do you want to tell them or shall I?"

We head to the reception and see a group of four people standing there looking confused as Marigold explains what happened. I look with interest at the new arrivals and see an extremely smart middle-aged couple standing behind an older couple, who look very concerned.

The man is looking agitated and says loudly, "What do you mean there's no staff? We've had this booked for close on a year and had no email telling us differently. Who's in charge around here? I want answers and fast."

Marigold looks uncomfortable and Leo steps forward and says coolly, "If I may interrupt."

The man looks at him and says dismissively, "And you are...?"

"Another guest and just as surprised by all of this as you are. We can't change what's happened, but you do have a choice."

"What choice? What are talking about?"

The man shakes his head with exasperation and the woman with him places her hand on his arm and says in a calm voice, "Hear the man out, Colin."

Leo says calmly, "Now, you can either choose to make the best of a bad situation and use the hotel and its facilities on a self-catering basis like the rest of us, or you can make a call and request a boat to take you home. There is really no other choice."

The man shakes his head angrily and I whisper, "What do you mean, call for another boat? I thought there was only one way off of here and it was on your scheduled day of departure."

Leo grins. "I had a chat with your friend Ryan when I was out for a run. He told me if anyone wants to leave, he has a boat that he uses to get to the mainland and can take anyone that wants to go. I'm sure he would oblige in the circumstances."

Before I can ask him when he saw Ryan, one of the women starts to cry and sobs, "I knew this would happen. It's a warning. I told you it wouldn't work."

We look in surprise as the man with her pulls her into his arms and strokes her hair, saying calmly, "There, there, it will all be fine. We've booked everything and left nothing to chance. This won't affect us because we have arranged everything ourselves."

She pulls back and smiles a watery looking smile. "Do you think so?"

He nods and I watch as he kisses her softly on the lips and says gently, "All you have to do is go and unpack and make yourself look even more beautiful than you are already."

He turns to Marigold and says firmly, "Please can you show us to the honeymoon suite? We booked it under the name of Mr and Mrs Fellowes."

Marigold looks sympathetic. "I'm sorry, but all bookings have been cancelled. It's now on a first-come, first-serve basis and I believe that room has already been taken."

I feel bad as I remember that Alice and Harold bagged the best room and the woman's eyes fill up once again as Marigold says hastily, "Listen, don't worry, there's an equally amazing room situated not far from that one. Give me thirty minutes or so and I'll prepare it for you. Why don't you make yourselves comfortable in the lounge and I'll arrange some tea and cake to be sent in? That goes for all of you and we will soon have this sorted out."

As the guests follow her, Leo says in a whisper, "Poor Marigold. This is turning into more work than she can be expected to shoulder on her own. Maybe we should have a word with the guests to cut her some slack."

I feel surprised by Leo's words. He doesn't strike me as a man who would consider Marigold's feelings, but there is a soft side to him that I like very much. Thinking back, I remember how kind he has been since I arrived. He has made me feel welcome and made sure I'm cared for. He hasn't complained and has just tried to deal with a bad situation in a positive way. I feel ashamed of myself for judging him harshly at every opportunity and smile. "I'll help Marigold. To be honest, I would love it. It's not really my style to sit around and be waited on, anyway. I'll go and get the tea ready and you can tell Marigold it's all in hand."

I turn to leave and Leo reaches out and grabs my arm. "Scarlett..."

"Yes, Leo?"

He smiles and for some reason, my heart flutters at the look he gives me. He appears kind of lost and vulnerable and I wonder what's going on inside his head as he shrugs and drops his arm. "Um... thanks. It's good of you to step up."

He turns to leave and I'm left wondering what he was really going to say because it was obvious something was playing on his mind.

As I head towards the kitchen, I think about what's happened since I got here. Every day is a new adventure and despite it all, I relish every moment. Now I have a purpose and it's to make this Christmas on Holly Island a very special one because it could be the last one we get to enjoy here.

CHAPTER 10

*N*ow that I've made up my mind, I set about things with a purpose. I make the tea and coffee and discover that Marigold has been baking again and fill a tray with thick slices of fruit cake and some homemade cookies. I quite enjoy myself playing at hotels and by the time I have deposited the tray in the lounge, I'm feeling quite good about myself.

Leo appears to have left and I expect he's holed up somewhere finishing his book, so I go in search of Marigold.

I find her preparing the room for the new couple, and she shakes her head as I join her. "Terrible business."

"What is?"

"That couple downstairs. They told me they had it all planned and are here to renew their wedding vows."

I stare at her in horror as she says sadly, "Between me and you, there's something not right there. I think something's happened because nobody reacts like that unless they are mentally unstable."

"I doubt that," I say, laughing. "They were just disappointed, that's all, and who can blame them? I'm sure I'd be devastated if my special trip was ruined."

Marigold shakes her head. "I've been around people for more years than I care to remember and mark my words. There's a story there. Anyway, I'm sure it won't be all bad. They told me they had booked a priest to visit on Christmas Eve to perform the ceremony and I'm sure he won't let them down."

I help Marigold make up the bed and think about the couple downstairs. It seems a little lonely, just the two of them, and then something occurs to me. "Marigold, you don't think they have hundreds of guests arriving between now and Christmas Eve, do you?"

She looks horrified. "Good, God, I hope not. Could you imagine it? No, we need to find out if that's the case and take steps to avoid it. It's one thing looking after a small group of people, but another thing operating at full capacity. Maybe you should go and find out."

I nod and move towards the door. "Leave it with me, I'll sort it out."

As I head downstairs, I think about the new arrivals. I hope they are the last because Marigold's right. At the moment we can cope - just but what if the hotel does fill up to capacity? It would be a free for all and we would probably run out of supplies in a couple of days. This could all end up as a mammoth disaster and I feel as if I have a headache coming on at the thought.

As I pass Alice and Harold's door, I hear giggling inside and smile. They appear to have taken everything in their stride and haven't complained once. Their situation is a little unorthodox but as they are both free agents, I can't see what the harm is. In fact, they make me feel even more desperate than I was already. They are enjoying life and living each day as if it's their last. I, on the other hand, am just making the best of a bad situation and it's not fair on Gregory or me. I still feel bad about the way I just upped and left, but the more time I spend here, the more I realise it was the right thing to do.

I reach the foot of the stairs and see Leo heading towards me, apparently in a hurry. Grabbing my arm, he steers me into a little room that appears to be some kind of office and says in a whisper, "Listen, I've been thinking and I feel bad for the other guests."

His words take me by surprise and then he says quickly, "It's supposed to be Christmas and we are on Holly Island. I think we should all go outside and see what we can find to decorate the place. There must be some holly around here somewhere hence the name and I'm sure we can find a tree to dig up and decorate."

"That sounds great. Count me in. I'd love to bring some festive cheer to the place and it may make everyone bond together a bit more. Shall I go and see who wants to tag along?"

He nods. "I'll help you and we can meet by the entrance in, say, fifteen minutes?"

I grin and feel the excitement sparking inside. I love Christmas and decorating a tree is right up my street.

Quickly, I head to the lounge and find the new guests tucking into the tea and cake looking a little better than they did before. They look up and I smile happily. "Listen, we're after volunteers to come and hunt for holly and things to decorate the place. Make it more Christmassy, you know, get into the spirit of it all. Would any of you like to come?"

I think I know my answer before they speak because they look extremely underwhelmed by the request. The couple who are renewing their vows look uncomfortable and the man says slowly, "Well, ordinarily we would love to, but we've just arrived and haven't even got to our room yet. I think we will have to sit this one out; it's been a very trying day already and I think we could do with a lie down if I'm honest. Fiona is tired and well, you know."

His wife smiles and nods. "Martin's right, we really should get settled in first. Maybe Brenda and Colin will help out."

I look at the next couple on my list and the woman says firmly, "Listen, ordinarily we would love to pull on our Barbour wellies and join you, but we will also have to pass. It's a shame though because we are rather expert at tree surgery and horticultural decorating. I trained in the art of floristry at none other than Kew Gardens and was considered the best in the class, so call me if you need any pointers. We would come, but Colin has a dodgy heart courtesy of the time he got tuberculosis in Malaysia when we were on a trek to find a lost village. I like to keep him wrapped in cotton wool most of the time these days for obvious reasons."

She smiles fondly at Colin, who nods. "Brenda's right, love. We'll leave it to the youth and spend the afternoon unpacking and settling in."

Feeling a little disappointed, I head off to my room to get my coat and boots. It's absolutely freezing outside and I'm not sure how much help I'll be with my ankle still feeling sore, but I'll be damned if I'm staying here when something so exciting is taking place. Maybe Leo had more luck.

Once I'm dressed for what looks like a polar expedition, I head off to find Leo. I find him looking a little pale, and he shakes his head as I approach. "It looks as if you had as much luck as me."

"Yes, sorry, nobody else fancied it. What was Harold and Alice's excuse?"

Leo looks a little traumatised if I'm honest and shivers and I know it's not from the cold before saying, "Um...they were having a siesta and didn't have the energy."

I stare at him, wondering why he looks so strange and he appears to collect himself and says with a cough, "Ok, um… it's just us then."

Suddenly, he looks concerned. "Are you sure you'll be up to it? You have sprained your ankle, remember?"

"How could I forget? No, it's fine, I won't let a little thing like that keep me from enjoying Christmas. You lead and I'll follow."

To my surprise, he reaches out and takes my hand. "Then allow me to help you and if it gets too much, yell and we'll come hobbling back."

As I follow him with my hand in his, it feels nice. That is, if you get past the huge ski gloves we are both wearing, which actually means we aren't anywhere near holding hands, just gloves really, but that doesn't matter. It feels nice because Leo is nice. Nice and devastatingly handsome. What a combination. I'm going to enjoy getting to know him and this is the perfect time to start.

CHAPTER 11

*T*he air is sharp and clear and feels like the purest air on earth. I suppose I've never thought of it before. Air is air but this is different. It fills my lungs and breathes energy into my soul. It takes my breath away and replaces it with love. I love this - Holly Island, the fresh air, the fact it's so unspoilt and the man I'm sharing it with. Maybe I don't actually love Leo, but I like him. He appears to be good company and has a willingness to make everything better, which then makes me feel like being a better person. Yes, Leo is one special guy who makes you want to rise to his level.

As we walk, I stare at the landscape with joy. The sky is now the most vibrant blue and there are just a few wispy white clouds scuttling across it. The seagulls shout for food and the waves crash to the shore because the wind is still making its presence known. I shiver a little as it finds a crack in my armour against the cold and chills my bare skin. Leo grips my hand a little tighter and shouts above the noise. "Are you ok? Say if you'd rather go back but I think I saw a suitable place around the next bend."

I feel surprised because Leo appears to know his way around already and I just nod because any words would allow the small bit of heat left inside me to escape.

As we turn the corner, I am relieved to see a small forest beckoning us inside and feel grateful for the shelter the trees will offer us.

As we walk down the frozen, muddy path, I look around at the bare branches of the trees and the barren forest floor devoid of any vegetation. Only the creaking of the branches as they dance in the wind follows us because any animals that live here must surely be tucked up somewhere warm and cosy for the winter in their burrows. Trying not to think of the roaring fire back at Holly Island hotel, I look around me with interest. To my right, I spy a holly bush looking splendid wearing its holly berries with pride and I nudge Leo. He follows my gaze and nods. "Good choice, Scarlett. I've brought some secateurs and a roll of bin bags so we shouldn't have any problem gathering it."

He produces the items from inside his huge coat and I shake my head. "You know, I never actually thought of the practical things we would need. Thank goodness one of us plans ahead."

He laughs and hands me the bag to hold. "What can I say? I used to be a boy scout. Don't worry, Scarlett, you're safe with me."

He winks and sets about snipping bundles of holly from its branches and I hold the bag out dutifully until it's filled.

We move on in search of a suitable tree and Leo says with interest, "Tell me about your boyfriend. What did you say his name was?"

Once again, I feel bad and say awkwardly, "Gregory Richardson. He's training to be an accountant and will do quite well, I'm sure. He's always been good with figures and leaves no stone left unturned. You know, he always goes further than most people and makes sure that everything is covered. His attention to detail is second to none and I'm in no doubt that he'll have his own company one day."

Leo smiles and I say quickly, "Your turn. What about your girlfriend?"

This time Leo looks awkward and says sadly, "Davina Havilland. I was introduced to her at a family lunch one day. Her father is an old friend of my father's and we were sort of thrust together. The next thing I knew, I was, shall we say, encouraged to ask her out on a date. I knew we had been set up because, to my family, connections mean everything. Her family owns the Starbright group, you know, the health club and spa chain that's appearing everywhere and my family thought it would be a match made in heaven. My father owns a bank and could be useful to Davina's family and she would become the wife I was expected to marry."

I feel a little unworthy as I walk beside him and don't know what to say. Leo's world is one I don't know the first thing about. I was brought up in a council house and went to the local secondary school. We had nothing and my father was out of work for a while, which meant I had to join the queue at lunchtime for free school meals. I resented my family because we didn't have much, but I still loved them and they always want what's best for me. Thinking about Leo's family makes me feel a little sad for him because it's as if they have it all planned out for him, despite what he wants.

He shakes his head and says wearily, "The trouble is, I don't love Davina. To be honest, I don't even like her. She's not like you - real."

Trying to lighten the mood, I quip, "Are you saying she's a plastic Barbie?"

He laughs. "Got it in one. In fact, I think she must use the same stylist because she has long, blonde hair, startling blue eyes and a figure that looks as if she has her food injected so that she doesn't stain her brilliant white smile. I'm pretty sure she had plastic surgery because most of the time, her expression never changes from being slightly surprised. Her lips look as if she's been stung on the mouth and her nose looks completely wrong on her face. I wonder if her makeup is tattooed on because it never changes and I'm pretty sure she's had other assets plumped up, if you get my meaning."

I stare at him in surprise and he grins and we can't help it and just burst out laughing. I feel a little bad because I don't even know her and say, "I'm sure she's nice inside though."

"Maybe, but to be honest, Scarlett, I gave up trying to find out."

We carry on walking and I feel intrigued and have to ask, "How come you got engaged then?"

"We didn't."

"Oh, I thought you said you were supposed to marry her, maybe I misheard."

Leo stops and looks at me with such a wretched expression I think I hold my breath. "She doesn't know, well, at least I hope she doesn't."

I feel confused, and he sighs. "Just before I came here, my father called me to his office and told me that he expected an announcement at Christmas. He was tired of me fooling around with nonsense, as he put it, and expected me to settle down and produce the next generation. He told me that if I married Davina, it would be a match made in heaven and I would struggle to do better."

I stare at him in shock and say sharply, "Just tell him no. It's your life and this sounds like something out of a novel. What century does your father live in?"

Laughing bitterly, Leo looks as if he has the weight of the world on his shoulders. "My family has always operated this way. My parents were encouraged to marry and, to my knowledge, every relation has also been guided in their choice of a partner. Even my sister Annabel was introduced to her husband Charles and went along with it for a quiet life. You see, my family are dinosaurs and if I buck the system, I'm likely to be disowned."

I feel a little bad for him because he looks so dejected, so I give his hand a squeeze and say softly, "Just do what's right for you, Leo. I'm sure your family wouldn't disown you just because you don't want to marry Davina. Blood counts for a lot and you're probably just fearing the worst."

I almost think Leo is about to say something else because he opens his mouth and then appears to think better of it. Instead, he says brightly, "What about that one?"

Looking to where he's pointing, I notice a beautiful fir tree standing proudly against the elements and I say softly, "It's perfect."

As we look at the tree, my eyes fill with tears and I say with a break in my voice. "Look at that tree, Leo. Despite the weather battling it from all sides, it stands straight and proud. It bends with the wind and adjusts to its environment. Be that tree, Leo, and don't let anyone tell you how to live your life. Stand firm and believe in your own choices and do what makes your heart happy."

I watch as Leo's eyes soften and he stares at me with a strange expression. He looks a little wistful, and yet I see a spark in his eyes that wasn't there before. Then he laughs and says firmly, "Then we must look for another tree. It would go against everything you just said if we take an axe to it now."

Laughing, I nod. "If you put it that way, it would be rather barbaric. Listen, I don't know about you, but I'd rather find a smaller one that we dig up roots and all and then re-plant after Christmas."

We head away from the little tree and as we walk, I no longer feel the cold. I don't feel my ankle throbbing and I don't feel guilty about coming here. Like Leo, I have some hard decisions to face and maybe we were both always meant to find each other. Two people from opposite sides of the track with a shared problem. Maybe we can help each other find our way out of a storm and, who knows, we may even survive it together.

CHAPTER 12

We head back to the hotel and Leo said that he would find Ryan and ask him to help dig up the lovely little tree we found. As we head inside, I see Marigold looking very agitated and look at Leo in alarm. "What's wrong with Marigold? You don't think more guests have arrived, do you?"

"I hope not. Come on, let's see if we can help."

Marigold stops when she sees us coming and runs her fingers through her hair with distraction. "Oh, hi guys, I don't suppose either of you could help me out. I've made dinner but I'm not sure if I can be in two places at once."

Leo looks confused. "What do you mean?"

"Well, the guests are waiting to be served, but the food will get cold if I dish it up and then carry it from the kitchen to the table. I need some willing hands to deliver the food quickly."

I feel a little annoyed on her behalf, but before I can speak, Leo says angrily, "Honestly, didn't anyone listen. It's not your job anymore, Marigold, and the sooner these guests accept that the better off we'll all be. I've had enough of this.

Leave it with me. Head back to the kitchen, or home, it doesn't matter. It's time we laid down a few ground rules."

He heads off, shaking his head angrily and Marigold stares after him in total shock. "Where's he going?"

"I'm not sure, but wherever it is, I want to see it."

We follow him to the lounge and see the six guests sitting at tables, looking as if they are seated at a restaurant. They have all helped themselves to drinks from the bar and look as if they are waiting for a waitress to take their order. Leo strides in and says loudly, "Just for your information, there are no staff here. If you want anything, you have to get it yourself."

The shock bounces off the walls as the guests look at him in disbelief and Brenda says, "I thought you were joking. I mean, I thought you meant that the majority of the staff had left, not all of them."

She looks at her husband. "My goodness, it's just like the time we were visiting Carrie Edwards at Triton House."

She turns and says loudly, "Lord and Lady Sutherland were in residence, and some sort of sickness bug struck the entire staff down. Took to their beds they did and only Carrie, Colin and I were spared. Well, you can imagine the problem we faced, but we rallied around for Queen and country and put on an amazing spread. You remember, Colin, don't you?"

Colin nods solemnly and Brenda beams with pride. "Lady Sutherland was so grateful and, quite frankly, begged me to join her staff. I had to let the poor dear down gently because she took quite a liking to me. It has to be said."

Colin nods and Fiona says quickly, "So what are you saying? We have to get our own food?"

Leo nods. "Luckily for us, Marigold has prepared dinner out of the goodness of her heart. If you want it, you need to head to the kitchen where she'll dish it up. Then we need to help clear it all away and tidy up. You know, we could all have a great Christmas if we just muck in together. There's certainly enough food and drink and we have a fine hotel with heat and light. It could be fun if we just all lend a hand."

Suddenly, Alice pipes up, "I think that sounds a smashing idea. I'm game."

I catch Leo's eye and he grins as Harold says loudly, "It reminds me of when we did a stint on the Pacific Ocean. All shipmates together, working like a well-oiled machine."

He looks at Leo and booms, "Jolly good show, young man. Count us in. Alice and I will take on bar tending duties. It will be our pleasure."

Fiona looks a little alarmed. "This wasn't how it was supposed to be. What are we going to do, Martin?"

He frowns and looks a little put out. "I don't think we have a choice, darling. Maybe we should offer to do the washing up and consider our options in the morning."

Fiona looks unhappy about his offer, but Leo quickly says, "Thank you. I'll make sure the fires have enough wood and will be in charge of providing the decorations. Scarlett and Brenda can transform this place into a Christmas grotto and Marigold, if she agrees, can take charge of the catering. Colin, if you don't mind, please can I ask you to help me and if we all keep our own rooms tidy, there should be no need for anybody to do any more than that."

Alice claps her hand together and giggles. "This will be such fun. Goodness, Harold, I ever expected such an adventure. I bet Hilary Gooding and Bert Talbot aren't having as much fun as this stuck in the New Forest in that treehouse."

I stifle a grin as they follow Marigold out to the kitchen and Leo whispers, "There, do you think they're up to it?"

Watching Fiona and Martin following the others, looking extremely put out, I shrug, "Who knows, it will be fun watching them though."

CHAPTER 13

*O*nce dinner is over and I help Marigold put the last of the dishes away, I say with interest, "I don't suppose you know where the hotel keeps its Christmas decorations? It struck me at dinner that they must have had some."

She nods. "Probably in the attic. I'll come with you if you like. It will be fun poking around up there for a bit."

I follow her up the staircase and say, "Where's Ryan? I haven't seen him in ages."

"He's working. He lives on the mainland and works at a vet's practice. He has a little flat over the top and only comes here on his days off, if he hasn't got a better offer."

I smile and think of the dashing young vet and picture his life. Unlike me, he probably has lots of fun and is inundated with friends and girls chasing him. He is not only lovely to look at, but a nice person too.

I can't help myself and probe a little deeper. "Does he have a girlfriend?"

Marigold laughs. "Too many. He's always been the same,

never happy with just one girl. He moves onto the next one quicker than the weather changes on this island."

I feel a little disappointed at her words. Ryan appeared to be perfect in every way and this newfound knowledge has tarnished the image a little.

Marigold stops outside a door located at the very end of the third-floor hallway and says with excitement, "Here we are. Goodness, I haven't been up here in years. I'm quite looking forward to seeing what they have stashed away."

Feeling a spark of excitement myself, I wait for her to go first and am glad she finds the light switch, which floods the dusty attic with a strange dull light. It's difficult to see everything because the attic appears to run the whole length of the building and most of it is hidden in shadows. I feel a little nervous as I tread carefully among the many boxes littering the floor and try to ignore the smell of damp that hangs in the air.

Cobwebs provide homes to what must surely be a strong spider community, and I shiver as I think about what lurks in the shadows.

Marigold looks around and says thoughtfully, "If I'm guessing right, they should be over to the left. I came up here once to fetch them and hope they were returned to the same place."

We step around overflowing boxes of what appears to be paperwork and old photographs and I hear her say triumphantly, "Here they are. Thank goodness for routine."

I blink in the dusty light and manage to make out several large boxes sitting forgotten on a shelf in front of me and watch as Marigold lifts one down and peers inside. "Ooh, look, Scarlett. This one must have thousands of baubles inside. Here, take it to the staircase and I'll grab another."

With a lot of groaning and huffing and puffing, we manage to teeter back across the decaying floorboards with our treasure and soon find ourselves out in the hallway again. I'm not going to lie. I feel quite relieved to be back on safe ground and as Marigold joins me, I say quickly, "Maybe we should enlist more help in getting the rest. It's a bit precarious up there."

Marigold nods and follows me back the way we came to open the box of delights and see what we've got.

We pass Harold on the way and he shouts, "Good God, let me help you with that."

We look at him gratefully, but all he does is walk in front of us holding the doors open as we pass through them. Marigold rolls her eyes and I try not to laugh as we follow him.

We reach the ground floor and head to the lounge and Fiona and Martin look up in surprise. "What have you got there?" Fiona says with interest, while Martin jumps up to help Marigold set the box down.

"Christmas decorations, we think," I say, puffing a little and they move closer and we all look inside the boxes with interest.

As we pull out the decorations, it's to calls of delight from all around the room. It's funny how such simple pleasures cause so much excitement and soon Fiona, Martin, Brenda and Colin are helping sort the baubles into neat little piles. Alice wanders in halfway through with a bottle of wine and some glasses and we spend a nice time drinking and chatting among ourselves.

Brenda holds up a clear glass bauble with holly inside and sighs, "This reminds me of when I trained as a glassblower. Skilled work, you know, it was quite something to learn, but I was considered one of the best in the class."

I stifle a grin as Marigold tries not to laugh and I look at Colin with interest. He is nodding and looks at Brenda with so much pride I wonder if her tales have some truth in them. I mean, they can't all be true, surely?

We soon have several neat piles of decorations and Brenda says with excitement, "What now?"

Marigold yawns and looks at her watch. "Well, I'm exhausted, so I think I'll head home. Scarlett knows where the rest are, so if you want to bring some more down, feel free."

She stands to leave and I feel worried. "You should have company back to your cottage to make sure you get there safely. It's very dark outside and…"

She laughs loudly. "And what, Scarlett? In case you've forgotten, we're on an island and unless the abominable snowman has decided to holiday here this year, I'm perfectly safe. I've lived here long enough to know my way home, so don't worry, I'll be fine."

I shrug but still feel a little bad and wish Leo was here. I'm sure he would walk back with her and I look at Martin pointedly and he says quickly, "I'll walk with you; I could do with some fresh air."

Marigold looks surprised and I smile at him gratefully as they head outside.

Jumping up, I say brightly, "Who fancies a hot chocolate?"

Several hands shoot up and Fiona says eagerly, "I'll help you."

I feel a little surprised because so far Fiona hasn't struck me as the helpful kind, but I'm glad of her company as we make our way to the kitchen.

As we walk, she sighs heavily and shakes her head. "You know, Scarlett, I knew something bad was going to happen."

"What do you mean?"

"Well, things have been a little difficult this last year or two and I suppose I'm so used to things going wrong, I kind of expected this to as well."

I say nothing but nod sympathetically and she says in a low voice, "This renewal of ours is the last chance. If this doesn't work, I think we'll have to admit defeat and go our separate ways."

She sounds so sad I stop and say softly, "I'm sorry to hear that."

Her eyes fill with tears and she sniffs. "It's all my fault. I made it this way and I don't deserve Martin, really I don't."

"Why, it can't be that bad, surely?"

She blinks and some tears fall down her cheeks as she says in a whisper, "I had an affair."

I stare at her in shock and she looks around her before lowering her voice. "It destroyed Martin. You see, it wasn't with a random stranger or anything, it was much closer to home."

I hold my breath as she says with pain in her voice, "It was his brother, Guy."

She looks at me with a mixture of pain and defeat and says in a small voice, "I told you it was bad. That's why we came alone. It's divided the whole family and when Martin vowed to stand by me, it caused a huge family rift."

"But why, surely, he's the injured party. Why wouldn't his family stand by him?"

"Because of me. You see, they hate me, Scarlett. They can't direct their hate at Guy because he's one of them. They blamed me for the whole sorry mess and told Martin to divorce me and get out as quickly as possible. I'm no longer welcome in the family and neither is he if he sticks by me. That's why I'm so emotional because I don't deserve a man like him."

Feeling upset for her, I reach out and hug her impulsively. She feels so slight and frail against me and my heart twists in pain for her. "Why did you, um... have the affair? It must have been for a reason. I mean, if you were happy together, I'm sure it would never have happened."

Pulling back, Fiona wipes away her tears with her fingers and shakes her head sadly. "I was weak and Guy was charming. Martin was away a lot with the airline he works for and Guy was having problems with his wife Sadie. He started coming around a lot and offloading his problems because he said I had a sympathetic ear. He started showing me attention and made me laugh. It felt good to laugh again and was just like old times."

I still don't understand how a woman could do what she did, but I smile and nod towards the kitchen. "Come on, whatever your reasons, they were valid at the time. Not that I'm an expert or anything, but I do know it takes two to make a marriage work, and yours was obviously at a turning point."

As I start to make the drinks, I can't help but ask, "How did Martin find out?"

She heaps the chocolate in several mugs and sighs. "He arrived home early and found us in bed together. Textbook really, but none the less devastating. I don't think I'll ever forget the look on his face. It destroyed him."

I feel sorry for Martin because it must have been a bitter blow to find his wife with his brother, not even a stranger, and my heart goes out to him.

Fiona sighs heavily. "If I could rewind my life and erase everything that happened, I would in a heartbeat. I suppose we all make mistakes, but that was the biggest one of my life. Faced with losing Martin, I realised how much I loved him. We talked it through and he decided to stick by me and give it another go. The renewal was his idea, even though I felt it was a bit soon. You see, Scarlett, this only happened a month ago. Do you think this is normal, I mean, to be committing ourselves again so soon?"

I'm not sure what to say because, if I'm honest, I do think they are rushing things a little, but I push my uneducated opinion aside and just smile. "I'm sure it's going to turn out for the best in the end. You're lucky that he loves you so much. It's like the sweetest love story and I think you are so lucky. If you love Martin, I think you should seize this opportunity to make things right with both hands and put the past behind you. I'm sure his family will come around. I mean, it's still raw, so they are reacting in the eye of the storm. Let the dust settle and then things may return to what they were, only better. Sometimes tests like these strengthen rather than weaken and you will look back on it as the time you faced your toughest test and won."

I know I'm babbling, but I'm not sure what else to say. I don't agree with what Fiona did and I do think they are rushing things, but she doesn't need to hear that from a stranger. If anything, she looks a lot happier and I breathe a sigh of relief for that, at least. As we walk back to the others, it strikes me that everybody here could be hiding from something, like me and Leo, come to mention it. Maybe we are all here on a remote island at Christmas for just that reason.

I watch as Harold and Alice make their way towards us, giggling and I smile. I doubt they are keeping any secrets. If anything, they are the most honest people here. At least they don't care what people think of them and are just enjoying life as best they can. I certainly hope I'm as full of life as they are when I'm their age. I wonder if I'll find someone to grow old with. I certainly hope so.

CHAPTER 14

*O*ver the next couple of days, life on Holly Island settles into a cosy routine. The guests all muck in and we manage to get by using the hotel as a rather nicely equipped home from home. I rarely see Leo because he is mainly holed up in his bedroom writing his book and the other guests have their partners, so things become a little lonely for me.

I spend my days walking around the lovely island exploring and my evenings are spent helping out in the hotel. We have managed between us to decorate the rooms with all the decorations we have found and have transformed the amazing hotel into a festive wonderland.

Today, the sun is shining, and the air is crisp and cool. As I set out for an early morning jog, I hear somebody calling my name and turn to see Leo following me and by the looks of him, he has the same thing on his mind – fitness. I swallow hard as I see the rather fit man jogging towards me and try to remember that I already have a boyfriend, who I am working out ways to let down gently just as soon as I return.

"Hey, Scarlett, do you fancy some company?"

I smile and jog on the spot to keep warm because it is seriously freezing out here in this clear sky. "Great, I'd like that."

We fall into step beside each other and Leo says happily, "I finished my book this morning."

"That's great; well done."

He nods. "Yes, the story's written, but now I need to start editing. That's a long process."

"You must be very pleased. What happens next?"

"I work just as hard at polishing it up and then send it off to publish."

We jog down the hill and I see the sea before us, looking beautiful this morning. The sun is reflected on the surface and little sparkles of light make it appear as if it's full of rare gems. Despite the cold, it feels warm because the exercise has caused the blood to rush through my veins and create a feeling of happiness inside. Either that or the fact my companion is unnaturally gorgeous.

For a minute, we stop and stare at the sea and just take in the beauty of it. As moments go, this one is special because I don't think I have ever been so at peace with myself. Here on Holly Island, life is easy and uncomplicated and my problems seem a world away. The people I am sharing the experience with are good fun. However, one in particular makes me look for him in a crowded room and causes my heart to flutter when I draw a smile from his heavenly lips. Now that man is staring at me with interest and I feel my face burn as he says softly, "Tell me about Gregory again."

"There's nothing much to tell. I need to finish with him, I know that but he's a lovely man and I feel bad about doing it. I suppose that's why I jumped at the chance to come here because Christmas is not the time to do it. It's meant to be a happy time and if I ended things with him, it would always be a reminder and I don't want that. Nothing should spoil Christmas, it's the law."

He grins and pulls me down on the ground next to him, and we look out across the bay. It feels good sitting next to him sharing this moment and then he says sadly, "You know, I am meant to leave today."

I stare at him in shock. "Leave, I didn't know that."

He nods and looks a little sad. "Yes, I was always only meant to be here for a few days before I'm due to return home and spend Christmas with my family. Davina will be there with her family and it's expected that I tie up the marriage proposal so the family can celebrate our engagement over the Christmas turkey."

I feel my heart take a tumble for the worse and try to say cheerfully, "So, this is goodbye."

He sighs heavily and turns to face me, and the look in his eyes makes me stop breathing.

"I don't want to go, Scarlett. I don't want to leave this place, the hotel and the people inside, but most of all, for some strange reason, I don't want to leave you."

My heart thumps as I gasp, "Me?"

Time stands still as he looks into my eyes and, like every romance novel I've ever read in the past, the moment couldn't be more romantic, as he says softly, "Yes, you. Ever since I first met you on the night of the storm, something about you called to my soul. That first night, I was confused about my feelings for a total stranger as I watched you sleep in the chair across from me. The flames from the fire illuminated your face, and I was mesmerised."

I swallow – hard.

"Then the more time I spent with you, the more you intrigued me. I wanted to spend every minute with you and when you were caught in the storm and didn't come back, I was frantic. I didn't understand why and yet when I saw you with Ryan, I felt so jealous I couldn't breathe."

My head spins as he looks into my eyes and says gruffly, "Now everything has changed, because I want to stay and get to know you more. I want you to be free to explore something that could be amazing with me and I want us to spend Christmas together but…"

He breaks off and I feel my heart lurch as I say tentatively, "But you can't. Is that what you're saying?"

He doesn't say anything and I realise this could be the only time I get to say what I feel in my heart, so I take a deep breath and say in a trembling voice, "Don't go, Leo. I don't want you to. This place wouldn't feel the same without you and for some reason… well, I have feelings for you too."

He looks at me quickly and a slow smile breaks out across his face as I watch all the worry evaporate before my eyes. "You do?"

I nod shyly and then, as the birds sing all around us like in the finest Disney movie, he leans towards me and as our lips touch, nothing else seems to matter. The chill in the air is replaced by warmth and the cold, hard ground under our feet becomes the most comfortable cushion as Leo's lips find mine.

As kisses go, this one is the best of my life because this one has feeling behind it. It's so romantic and for a woman who spends more time reading about it than actually experiencing it, this is going in my memory book - sharpish.

Leo reaches out and pulls me closer, and it's as if we can't breathe without the other as we kiss relentlessly. Our bodies touch and I feel my heart thumping inside as I savour the moment. Now I understand what all those books were written about. Possibly this isn't the right time to think about it, but I can't help but compare it to kissing Gregory. Now I know I was right to pull away from him because the feelings inside me are far more powerful as I kiss Leo. I actually feel so euphoric I never want to stop.

However, all too soon, he pulls away and I smile shyly as he says gently, "I knew it would be you."

"Me?"

"Yes, you. The woman I was meant to find."

He puts his arm around my shoulder and pulls me close, and I don't feel anything but warm inside. Leo laughs softly and I say, "What's so funny?"

"Do you know what today is?"

"No."

He grins. "Departure day."

"I don't understand."

He laughs and jumps up, pulling me with him. "We get to meet the man who's responsible for taking us off the Island. I don't know about you but I'm keen to meet him, even if it is to tell him he has no passengers."

I stare at him with hope and say tentatively, "You're not leaving."

He pulls me close and whispers, "No, Scarlett, why would I leave when we are about to start something amazing?"

I feel my heart racing as I say softly, "But what about your family - Davina?"

He shrugs. "What about them? I'm old enough to make my own decisions and if it means I upset them, I couldn't care less."

"But what about your job, your family, won't it affect everything?"

Laughing, Leo swings me up into his arms and kisses me hard before saying, "It doesn't matter because I don't need any of it."

He sets me down and says earnestly, "Spend Christmas with me, Scarlett. Let's enjoy the next week or so and then face our problems together."

I nod as he takes my hand and starts pulling me quickly behind him, "Come on, we have things to do."

As we start running back towards the hotel, I feel freer than I have ever felt in my life. Here on Holly Island real life doesn't drag you down. It stands aside and lets the amazing in for just a short, fantastic, moment. Can we hold on to this feeling? I certainly hope so because Leo was right about one thing, I felt the same connection with him and I'm excited to see where it leads.

CHAPTER 15

*O*nce we have showered and changed, Leo and I meet up and head towards the jetty in search of the elusive 'departure boat'. Check out time is 11.00 am on Holly Island, so we are certain not to have missed it.

As we walk, we talk and discover we have many shared obsessions. We both love the gym and endless walks. We like going to the cinema and, of course, reading. We also share a passion for travel. However, in my case, it's the wish I could and in Leo's because it has always been a part of his life. For the first time in what appears to be forever, I feel hopeful for the future and am looking forward to the New Year and am interested to see where it takes me.

As we wait for the boat, Leo and I stand on the jetty and huddle together to keep warm. We share many long, lingering kisses and my heart is so full I worry something will come along to cause it to burst.

On the dot of eleven, we hear the distinct sound of an outboard engine, and I look at Leo with excitement. "He's here."

We turn our attention to the horizon and see the small boat approaching, and then look at each other in confusion.

"This can't be right." Leo looks again and says, "Surely not."

I strain to see what he can and turn to him in surprise. "That looks like Hagrid's boat and he appears to have people on board."

"Hagrid?"

I giggle. "I don't know his actual name but he reminds me of Hagrid in Harry Potter, although a lot more unrefined."

Leo laughs. "Even more unrefined than Hagrid, that's saying something."

He looks surprised and says in confusion, "I thought he only did arrivals."

"Me too, maybe his brother is ill or something."

We watch as the boat approaches and look with interest at the new arrivals. I'm getting quite used to seeing people arrive and wonder what they will think of the fact they have paid to stay on a deserted island. I watch with interest as a family of four arrives alongside the jetty and the man smiles and throws Leo the rope to pull them in.

As soon as their boat is tethered, the man jumps ashore and holds out his hand. "Pleased to meet you, I'm Kevin Harris, and this is my family."

Leo smiles. "Hi, I'm Leo and this is Scarlett. We're staying here too."

Grinning, the man points to a woman who is trying to steer a little boy towards the jetty and Kevin grabs his hand and hauls him out of the boat, saying, "Meet Jamie, my son."

Jamie looks at us with wide, angelic eyes and smiles a crooked grin. I think he must be only around five years old and my heart melts as I see the excitement in his eyes. Crouching down to his level, I say kindly, "Hi, Jamie, welcome to Holly Island."

He nods shyly before hiding behind his father as a young girl jumps out, pointedly ignoring the hand her father offers her. She scowls all around as Kevin laughs softly, "This is Rebecca."

I smile and she nods before looking down at her phone and sighing. "Still no reception. Where are we, outer Mongolia?"

The woman jumps to shore and rolls her eyes, "Teenagers, they can't live without their phones for five minutes."

She holds out her hand and says warmly, "Hi, I'm Phoebe."

As I shake her hand, I note the friendliness in her eyes and feel happy with the new arrivals. They look normal enough and it will be good to have some younger people around, hopefully with no excess baggage.

Leo turns to Hagrid and says quickly, "I thought the departure boat would be here."

He just shrugs. "No departures today, only arrivals."

Leo shakes his head. "No, you're mistaken. I was booked to leave today and to my knowledge haven't told anybody to the contrary."

The man starts untying the boat and pushes it back from the jetty after making sure all the family's luggage is safely deposited onshore.

"No departures today," is all he says as he rows away from the jetty. As Leo begs to differ, the sudden roar of the outboard engine cancels any further conversation and we watch with considerable surprise as the boat heads back the way it came.

"For goodness' sake, I can't even get 3g let alone 4g. What is this place? There had better be Wi-Fi otherwise I'm swimming back to civilisation."

Spinning around, I watch with amusement as Rebecca

storms off down the jetty, holding her phone up in disgust, searching for any available signal, and Phoebe sighs. "This could end up being a very trying trip."

Kevin shakes his head as Jamie yells, "Hurry up daddy, do you think there's treasure on this island? Can we find it, can we do it now?"

He tugs at his father's arm and we look with amusement as Phoebe laughs softly, "At least one of our children is happy to be here."

We help them with their luggage and as Leo and Kevin lead the way, I fill Phoebe in on what to expect. She looks utterly horrified as she discovers that their holiday is about to go from bad to worse. "What, no staff at all? You're kidding me?"

Shaking my head, I say gloomily, "I'm not and what's more, I'm sorry to say there's no Wi-Fi."

Phoebe looks at me in horror as I shrug. "Apparently, the storm we had a few days ago knocked the satellite out and we've had no communications ever since I arrived. No television, no internet and no phone. I'm sorry Phoebe, I don't know how you're going to break it to Rebecca."

She groans and I see the worry enter her eyes. "This is a disaster. Not for us, quite frankly I couldn't care less if we have no communication, but it was hard going persuading Rebecca to come at all. To be honest, it's been a difficult few months, and it was touch and go whether she would come with us."

She looks so miserable and my heart sinks. Great, more problems to add to the mix.

We near the hotel, and Phoebe looks up at the magnificent place and smiles. "It looks as good as it did in the advert. Maybe it won't be so bad. We're only here for a week and it will probably do us all good to get back to basics for a while."

Laughing, I wave my hand around. "It's not that basic,

really. Despite everything, it is still luxury. I must warn you though, the other guests are a little eccentric."

Phoebe laughs. "Then we should fit in just fine."

As she walks inside, I catch sight of Leo helping Kevin with the luggage and feel a warm feeling inside. This place is perfect, to me anyway, because he's here. Today is the first day of the rest of my new amazing life and I can't wait to see where that leads.

CHAPTER 16

*O*nce the new arrivals have chosen their rooms, I head back downstairs with Leo. We meet Brenda and Colin heading our way and smile warmly, and I don't miss the knowing looks they share as they see Leo's hand firmly in mine.

As they draw near, Brenda says loudly, "Just the people I was looking for. You know, I was thinking…."

Colin laughs. "Dangerous pastime of hers, prepare yourselves."

She rolls her eyes and says quickly, "Now, I don't know about you, but I love Christmas and want to make this a good one. I've decided we should all pull together and take charge of one aspect of the Christmas festivities. I am calling a meeting for later on this afternoon in the resident's lounge. We need to take ownership of this and make plans for the best Christmas day we've ever had."

She looks at us for approval and I am keen to give her mine, at least. "I love that idea. You can count me in."

Leo nods. "Me too."

Brenda lowers her voice. "You know it was lucky for

everyone that I came. I'm quite good at organising events, just ask the Beatles."

She laughs and looks very pleased with herself. "Yes, I was instrumental in their success back in the day. I worked at the record label and was called upon to organise many a soiree with other famous names. My parties were the stuff of legends and I could have made quite the career out of it. Oh well, happy days and now I must put my skills to the test once again and apply them here. Come along, Colin, we need to go and have our usual constitutional around the ornamental gardens and brainstorm in readiness for this afternoon's session."

Colin grins as they walk past and Leo shakes his head. "You know, I'm not sure if Brenda is just the most fantastic liar I have ever met or the most fantastic person. Even if half of her stories are true, she's a legend."

Giggling, I have to agree with him. "You don't meet many people like Brenda in life and I am choosing to believe every word she says."

We head towards the kitchen to fix ourselves a nice, warm drink and find Marigold elbow deep in flour. There's a mouth-watering scent of baking that causes my stomach to growl and she smiles happily. "Just in time, I need someone to grab those muffins from the oven."

Quite prepared to beat Leo off with a rolling pin, I race towards the oven gloves and prepare myself to savour the enticing aroma of muffin perfection.

Marigold shouts, "Leo, put the kettle on, will you? I'm gasping for a cuppa."

He does as he's told, and I fill Marigold in on the new arrivals.

"Goodness, this place is filling up at an alarming rate. Who knew it would be so busy?"

"Is it too much for you?"

She laughs incredulously. "No, to be honest, I thrive on it. You know, I was thinking, and I ran it past Ryan and he agreed."

Leo looks interested, "What?"

"I think I'll move in here while there are guests. There's plenty of room and then I can carry out my chores without the need to run my own home. It will be fun and I could use the company."

She smiles and I note the excitement in her eyes and feel happy for her. It must be quite lonely and she is obviously thriving on all of this, so I nod. "I think that's a great idea. Watch out for Harold though, he's got his eye on you."

I laugh as she blushes prettily and shakes her head. "Enough with your teasing. He has more than enough to handle with Alice."

We all laugh and as Leo hands us each a mug of tea, Marigold hands us a muffin to try. "Here, we may as well sample the goods. It's the cook's prerogative. Yes, I think that will be the best thing all round and I'll get Ryan to help me with my suitcase later when he gets back."

Through a mouthful of cake, I mumble, "Is he at work?"

She nods. "Yes, as usual. I wish he didn't work so hard, but there's no telling him. Anyway, maybe he will have some time off at Christmas and we can all spend it together. Now, tell me, things are looking a little different since yesterday. What happened?"

We stare at her in surprise and she grins. "Nothing gets past me, and I noticed that you both appear a little closer. Care to fill me in?"

Leo laughs and reaching out, takes my hand and raises it to his lips. "I found what I've been looking for and I hope that Scarlett has too."

Marigold's eyes fill with tears. "I'm so happy for you both."

As she wipes her eyes, she says almost to herself, "Holly Island weaves an intricate web of magic that is hard to escape. I'm glad it worked for you."

Leo and I share a look and my heart fills with happiness. "I think it did, Marigold. I think Holly Island did its job just fine."

After filling our stomachs with more muffins than is healthy to eat, Leo and I decide to head off for a walk. There isn't much else to do here unless we decide to play a board game or cards. Some of the guests found an ageing DVD player and I think Top Gun is showing today because I see Fiona and Martin wrapped in each other's arms, cuddling up on the sofa watching it as we pass.

I fill Leo in on what she told me, and he shakes his head. "That's tough. I'm not sure if I could be so forgiving."

I have to agree with him because, in my eyes, it was the ultimate betrayal. We hear the sound of laughter nearby and see Kevin playing chase with Jamie, and Leo smiles wistfully. "He's so lucky."

"Who, Jamie?"

"Yes." Leo grins. "My father never played with me. In fact, I was always made to be seen and not heard, until I was useful, of course."

"Useful?"

He nods sadly. "He only showed an interest when I graduated from university. Then it was full steam ahead getting me installed at the company working under my uncle."

"What does your father do?" I say with interest, but from the look on his face I wish I'd never asked.

"He runs the company. He's the chairman and my uncle's the managing director. My grandfather set the company up and as my father's the eldest, he got the top job when he died. They think they're royalty in my family and only the immediate heir gets to run things. So, when my father retires or dies, that honour will fall to me, even though I have two other cousins who would long to take charge."

I feel sorry for him. "And you don't?"

"No." He looks so upset I almost want to cry and he says sadly, "I just want to write and to live a simple life where there are no corporate meetings and bottom lines to achieve. I want to enjoy travelling and to be happy and in love. Is that too much to ask?"

Reaching for his hand, I squeeze it gently. "No, that's not too much to ask. In fact, it sounds perfect in every way."

We stop walking and share yet another kiss, and everything in my world is perfect. We have a week to push aside any important decisions and just enjoy a time when life is good in every way.

As we resume our walk, I ask the question that's been burning on my tongue ever since I discovered what Leo did. "Am I allowed to read one of your stories?"

I don't miss that he tenses up and says with distraction, "Maybe one day, but the one I've got here is as rough as sandpaper. I wouldn't want you to see it in its unpolished form. Maybe when it's finished."

I smile but feel a little disappointed. I would love to read what he has written because if it's anything as amazing as he is, it's sure to be a bestseller. In my eyes, anyway.

CHAPTER 17

*B*renda's voice rings out, "I have gathered you all here to discuss the logistics of Christmas."

I almost laugh out loud at the faces around me as they look at Brenda with extreme apprehension. She is standing at the front of the room holding a clipboard, looking extremely official.

I laugh to myself as I see Rebecca staring angrily at her phone as Jamie plays with a handheld computer. Fiona and Martin look bored and Harold and Alice are drinking what appears to be double shots of brandy. Colin is looking proudly at his wife, and Phoebe catches my eye and grins as Marigold flicks an imaginary speck of dust from the sideboard.

"Ok, I have a list of jobs that need names beside it, so I'll start the ball rolling. I'll put myself down as the event organiser and Colin will do his magic tricks."

I daren't look at Leo as Brenda scribbles on her clipboard and then looks over her spectacles, saying, "Any more acts to list?" She looks at Harold. "What about you, Captain? What are your talents?"

Alice giggles as Harold winks, before saying, "I can recite a few verses of poetry if you like."

Rebecca mumbles, "Kill me now."

I stifle a grin as Brenda looks at me and says, "Scarlett, what are your talents?"

Leo laughs as I say rather red-faced, "I could sing if you like."

Brenda nods before turning to Leo, "And you, what can I put you down for?"

Leo looks alarmed and then sighs, "I can play the piano."

Brenda looks pleased as Jamie pipes up, "I can do my impression of a fart if you like."

His parents look horrified as he demonstrates the art of making noises with his armpits. Brenda looks slightly bemused and then smiles. "Jamie and his amazing talking body it is then."

Kevin laughs out loud as Phoebe rolls her eyes and then the smile is wiped off his face as Brenda says to Rebecca, "What about you, my dear, what talents can you offer?" Rebecca looks horrified. "Count me out. I won't be here, anyway."

The room falls silent and she shrugs. "Well, I won't. As soon as I get a signal, I'm calling mum to come and get me. Quite frankly, it can't come soon enough for me."

"Rebecca!"

Kevin speaks angrily and Phoebe lays her hand gently on his arm and says softly, "It's ok. Leave her."

The atmosphere turns a little awkward until Martin says loudly, "Fiona and I can demonstrate our ballroom techniques. We are avid watchers of Strictly and even went to a few classes last year."

Fiona looks mortified as Brenda scribbles it down.

Then she turns to us all and says lightly, "Now, I have taken the liberty of assigning you all roles to avoid arguments. Before you object, it's the best all-round and saves disagreements. Feel free to swap if you'd rather but make sure to keep me informed. Now, I am in charge of event coordination, as I said before. Colin is in charge of keeping the fires stocked along with Leo and doing any heavy lifting or maintenance. Scarlett, you are responsible for decorations and making sure the Christmas table looks magical. Fiona, you are on cleaning duty and Phoebe, you can help Marigold with the food preparations. Alice and Harold appear to enjoy playing at bar tending, so are responsible for making sure the wine flows and nobody overindulges."

She peers over her spectacles at them and says firmly, "That includes both of you."

Then she looks at Kevin and winks. "We'll need a Santa Claus so that honour falls to you. Now, have I missed anyone out?"

"Me."

We look up in surprise to see Ryan standing in the doorway, looking extremely handsome. I don't miss the fact that Rebecca's eyes light up as Marigold says loudly, "You're home."

He nods and then produces the most adorable bundle of delight from behind his back and the sound of gasps of pleasure can be heard around the room as we stare at the most gorgeous puppy blinking in his arms.

The little black dog looks only to be a few months old and his tail wags as he regards the room with black, compelling eyes.

Ryan grins and says proudly, "Meet Jasper. He needs a home this Christmas, and I didn't want to leave him locked in a cage at the local dog pound. Maybe he can share his Christmas with us instead?"

Marigold smiles happily as, one by one, the guests crowd around to welcome Jasper.

Ryan pops him down on the floor and Jamie looks at him with such a delighted expression it melts my heart as Ryan says to him, "Can you look after him for me?"

Jamie's eyes are as wide as saucers as he nods and then turns to his mother, "Can I mummy?"

Phoebe looks a little unsure and says reluctantly, "Only while we're here, Jamie. You do know we can't keep him."

Rebecca rolls her eyes and kneels down next to her brother. I watch as she extends a hand to Jasper's nose and waits patiently for him to sniff her fingers before stroking his soft, silky head. She smiles at Jamie and says in a sweet voice, "He likes you, Jamie."

I watch as Jamie looks so happy it melts my heart and Rebecca smiles at her brother and at this moment, I see what a beautiful young lady she is. Gone is the surly teenager with the weight of the world on her shoulders and in its place is a kind, caring sister who obviously loves her brother very much. She raises her eyes to Ryan, who can't appear to take his own off her and says softly, "May I?"

He nods and we watch as she lifts Jasper onto Jamie's knee and the two of them pet the little puppy until its tail wags so hard it may take off.

I watch their parents as they share a look and can tell that one simple act means the world to them.

Ryan stands and moves next to his mother as Brenda clears her throat and says gruffly, "Ok, that's all settled then. Now, as we all know, we have been placed in a situation out of our control and will have to pull together to make this work. There will be no slacking and no complaints. We work as a team and then everyone's happy. Now, I will be running a gift making class tomorrow if anyone is interested in joining me. I don't know about you but I love to give gifts at Christmas and this is no exception. In the absence of any shops, we will have to pool our skills to come up with something the rest may enjoy."

She turns to Harold and Alice. "Why don't you both organise some drinks in the bar and we can toast our new venture? Thank you all for listening and let's make this a Christmas to remember."

We all clap as she takes a seat, and the meeting breaks up as everyone starts their own private conversations. I watch with interest as Ryan joins Rebecca and Jamie, who are obviously enamoured of the puppy and I see that the light has returned to Rebecca's eyes.

Leo whispers, "Ryan saved the day a bit there."

I watch him laugh at Jasper and nod. "He has a habit of doing that."

"What do you mean?"

"I don't know, maybe because he always seems to be there when he's needed."

Leo nods and then pulls me to my feet and grins. "Come on, let's go and get a drink. We may as well start the festivities early; it is Christmas, after all."

We head to the bar and I think about what Brenda has done. Genius really. She did exactly the right thing because we needed guiding in the right direction. Maybe she is this superwoman and can lend her hand to everything. I like to think she is, anyway.

$\mathcal{L}$eo and I have far too much to drink, along with most of the other guests. Alice and Harold pour extremely large measures and even Fiona is giggling with Colin in the corner while Brenda dances the can-can with Martin. Ryan and Rebecca are settling Jasper into his new home with Jamie supervising, and Phoebe and Kevin are dancing the waltz to the tune of the rusty old gramophone that Marigold found in the attic.

Leo whispers, "Come with me, Scarlett."

He pulls me from the room and, giggling, I follow him towards the front door. Grabbing some padded coats from the hall cupboard, he lifts his finger to his lips and slurs, "Shh."

Giggling, I follow him outside and feel the cold, crisp air almost instantly freeze me and I find I can't stop laughing as he pulls me towards the edge of the lawn. As we run through the trees, I try to catch my breath as the wind stings my cheeks and then, before I know what is happening, Leo pushes me against a tree trunk and kisses me relentlessly.

I kiss him back equally desperately until he murmurs,

"I've wanted to do that all evening. It's one thing socialising with the other guests, but there's only one I want to get to know more."

His eyes sparkle in the moonlight and I catch my breath. Leo wants me, really wants me, it's there in his eyes. He's looking at me with desperation mixed with lust, and I feel my legs tremble as I understand exactly what he wants.

He groans against my lips, "What are you doing to me?"

His words sober me up instantly as I realise where this could be heading because one thing I know is - I want him too.

As my head spins, I struggle to get a grip. Do I want this, I mean, really want Leo? I think I do, but how do you know? I've only ever been with one man before in my life, and that's Gregory. Even that was after several months together and I certainly didn't feel this carnal lust for him that I'm feeling now.

Leo presses his lips to mine and I kiss him back, matching him in every way. Every book I have ever read plays this scene out somewhere or another, but I'm beginning to wonder if this is a little early in the story for us. Am I that person? The one who throws caution to the wind and sleeps with a man after just knowing him for a week or so. Is this your typical holiday romance which will end as a delicious memory when the euphoria wears off?

Leo groans and whispers, "Shall we go somewhere more comfortable?"

The panic hits me fast and my head struggles to keep up. Oh my god, what's the right answer here? Do I keep my dignity and cool this down before things get out of control? If I let him, will he think badly of me, or if I don't, will he be disappointed? More than ever, I wish I had a phone signal because I need advice and fast. Rita will know what to do, but she isn't an option right now and so my heart beats frantically as I say with a slight tremor to my voice, "Ok."

He pulls back and I note the excitement in his eyes as he says softly, "You do?"

I nod shyly and he leans towards me and kisses me so gently I feel weak at the knees. Then he takes my hand and whispers, "Come with me."

My heart beats so frantically I wonder if it will give out and the doubts argue with my impetuous self all the way. What am I doing? This is madness. We have had far too much to drink for this to be a good decision. The trouble is, I want this - I want him. I don't care if it is foolish and reckless. I don't care if I look cheap and available. I don't give a damn if I am judged harshly because I have lived in the shadow of my reckless self for far too long. Scarlett Robins needs to grow up and take charge of her life and I know what Rita would say – go for it.

We sneak inside and head for the stairs looking like a couple of burglars. Silently, we scale the staircase and Leo holds my hand tightly, probably in case I change my mind.

My heart hammers inside, reminding me this is unusual and a bit dangerous, for me, anyway. We reach the door to Leo's room and he turns to face me, looking anxious. "Are you sure about this, Scarlett?"

I swallow hard and say in a weak voice. "I think I am."

He frowns, and I feel annoyed that I'm so weak and so I push my fears aside and lean forward and brush my lips against his. "I know I am."

With his lips on mine, he reaches for the door handle and as the door opens, we crash into the room. He slams it behind him and then, to my surprise, he pulls back and says huskily, "I won't be a minute."

I watch as he disappears into the bathroom and lick my

lips nervously. This is awkward. In fact, now I'm here, I'm completely sober and feeling like a fish out of water.

I look around and try to clear my head by taking some deep breaths, and then I see Leo's laptop open on the desk by the window. My curiosity overpowers my better judgement, and I wander over and see what appears to be a chapter of Leo's book on the screen. Looking around me furtively, I check the coast is clear and start reading.

As the words register with the one part of my brain that appears to be functioning, I feel my heart thump. This can't be right. The more I read, the hotter I get as Leo's words jump off the page. This isn't romance - it's pornography. Still, I keep reading because now I've started, I can't stop because the woman described in what appears to be the throes of passion is the spitting image of me.

I hear the toilet flush and am brought back to my situation as if a cold bucket of ice has been thrown at me and I don't even think - I run. Run from the situation, run from what was sure to happen and run from my feelings because that book… it was describing me and I'm not stupid and I was about to re-live the action right there in that room.

I can't deal with it and need to distance myself from the situation because if that's romance, I've been reading the wrong books.

CHAPTER 19

*M*y face is on fire as I take the stairs two at a time. I can't possibly go to my room because that will be the first place Leo looks. What am I going to tell him? I can't believe that just happened. I feel hot and sweaty and realise I'm probably having a panic attack. That was so unexpected and now I'm running with nowhere to go. What will Leo think when he sees I've gone? Will he know I've read his forbidden book, although now I can see why he was reluctant to show me? Was that girl he described really me? Is that all I am, a muse, a character outline, and was he going to re-live the pages he wrote for real?

I groan as I try to shut out the images that now won't go away and without thinking; I wrench open the door to the little office and lock it from the other side.

Taking a seat, I place my head in my hands and try to get my breathing under control. Wow. As evenings go, this one is up there as the strangest of my life.

As I contemplate what just happened, reasoning sets in. Maybe I overreacted, maybe it wasn't his book, and maybe that woman wasn't me. Perhaps Leo just intended to kiss a little more and my dirty mind has overstepped the mark. How will I explain the reason why I left and how on earth can I ever face him again now that I know what he does?

It's only as I open my eyes something swims into focus and I pounce on it like a lifebelt in a raging sea. The telephone.

I doubt we have a connection, but I have to try at least, so I grab it with an eagerness that shows me how pathetic I am and dial Rita's number, just hoping I remembered it correctly.

After a few rings, she answers sounding a little sleepy and I feel bad because I know she has to get up early in the morning.

"Who is it?"

"Rita, It's me, Scarlett."

"Oh my God, Scarlett, what's happening? Tell me you've found true love and are living in a castle somewhere."

I say in a rush, "Much, much, worse."

"Worse?"

"I've met someone and just nearly had sex with him in his hotel room."

"Whaaat!!!"

Her scream almost deafens me and then she says in confusion,

"What do you mean... nearly?"

"Well, it's a long story, but the man in question, and I mean MAN, is a writer, among other things. Well, after we crashed into his room, intent on getting to know each other on a more intimate level, he had to answer the call of nature. Well, unsure what to do with my time, I saw his laptop open on his desk with what appeared to be his latest book on it for all to see. Now, I know I shouldn't but the curiosity dragged me over there and I started reading."

"Slow down, Scarlett. You're incoherent. What do mean, among other things?"

"Never mind the finer details, the thing is, when I read it, I was shocked because apparently, this MAN writes pornography and described me in the starring role."

Rita gasps and then says with amusement.

"You lucky cow."

"Yes, well, I thought you'd say that, but I panicked. I mean, what if I was supposed to follow some sort of script and act out the pages on the screen? I'm no porn star, Rita, and quite honestly, he may be super-hot and all, but he's still well… depraved, surely?"

Rita bursts out laughing and I feel a little annoyed by it. I'm pouring out my heart, along with all my fears and dashed hopes and dreams, and she thinks it's hilarious.

Then she says with barely concealed amusement.

"So, what's your problem?"

"I think that's obvious, don't you?"

"No."

"Well, aside from the fact that I'm a few fumbles away from being a virgin because Gregory was hardly Christian Grey, I'm a little inexperienced, shall we say? Also, regarding the aforementioned Gregory, I am still his girlfriend and not the cheating kind. What sort of person cheats on her almost fiancé with a man that probably models himself on Hugh Hefner, God rest his soul? Not this romance loving, Gone With The Wind, historical romance, bookshop obsessive. No, it is so wrong on every level."

There's a pause and then Rita says a little awkwardly.

"Um… Scarlett, honey, I think there's something you should know."

Immediately the alarm bells start deafening me as I hold my breath and say quickly, "Oh my God - what? Is it mum, dad, the mouse? Oh, please not the hamster. I couldn't bear to think of Dobby lying injured somewhere. It's not Mr Saracen, is it, or the woman who lives at number 10? Please don't tell me Brexit has actually happened and I couldn't bear it if they cancelled University Challenge. Oh no, what about Gregory? Did he discover that I took the jumper he bought me for my birthday to the local charity shop? Please tell me it's none of those."

"It's none of those."

I breathe a sigh of relief and she laughs softly.

"Brownie points for placing Gregory last on your 'care for list.' Kudos to you."

"Just tell me, Rita, I'm having a panic attack on top of a panic attack here and I may not have long to live."

"I think Gregory's got another girlfriend."

Silence reigns and all I can hear is my heavy breathing as I struggle to understand the words she's just spoken.

Gregory. Has. Another. Girlfriend.

Of all the things I expected, that was never in the equation. Gregory is cheating on me! Ok, I have too, but that's not the point. The point is, he was going to propose marriage to me - wasn't he?

Suddenly, I'm not so sure and think back to the stilted conversations that have become the norm over the last few months. The fact we spend even less time together, which I thought was due to his extensive hobby list. Maybe he met her at one of his train spotting clubs. Then again, she could be a member of the Game of Thrones appreciation society he set up at the cricket pavilion on Thursday evenings. I wonder if they met in the library when he was researching life on Mars, or perhaps she works with him in the council offices organising his spreadsheets.

"What do you mean, you think he has another girlfriend?"

"Um... well, it may be because I saw them walking hand in hand when they joined the queue for the cinema to watch the

Christmas edition of Downton Abbey. It could be when he kissed her in broad dusk-light in full view of the public and it could be because my mum told me."

"Your mum?"

"Yes, she works in the council building with the girl in question. Fanny Burbridge is her name, and she works in care in the community."

"Fanny Burbridge! Good god, she sounds like one of the characters in Leo's book."

"Leo?"

"Yes, Leo, keep up Rita. Leo is the man upstairs polishing his imagination as he waits for me."

Rita laughs. *"Then what are you waiting for? Gregory appears to have moved on and, by the sounds of it, you've got a golden opportunity waiting for you. Tell me, Scarlett, is he good looking?*

"Very."

"Is he good company?"

"Extremely."

"Is he single?"

"Work in progress."

"What do you mean, work in progress?"

"Same as me, he has an engagement to break off."

"He's engaged!"

"Not yet."

"Then how can he break off something that's not a reality? It doesn't make sense."

"It's a long story."

"Ok, does he make you happy?"

"Extremely."

"Do you fancy him?"

"Terribly."

"Would you like a relationship with him?"

"More than anything."

"Is he rich?"

"I think so."

"For god's sake, Scarlett, get your ass up there and rip off your clothes as you go. I can't believe you're even having doubts. Go forth and enjoy and remember to tell me all the gory details tomorrow, preferably when I have a stiff drink in my hand and the computer open on executivematch.com."

Then, in a softer voice, she says, *"I miss you, babe. I just want you to be happy and by the sounds of it, this man - Leo, did you say, could be the one to do it. If things don't work out, at least you had the magic for a moment in time. Just enjoy yourself and try to have the best Christmas possible."*

"Thanks, Rita. I miss you too."

My voice sounds weak and vulnerable even to my own ears, and then it hits me. I'm free. I'm actually free and I don't have any emotional baggage to drag back upstairs with me. Suddenly, I feel excited and can't quite believe I'm still sitting here.

Quickly, I say, "Happy Christmas, Rita, sorry I've got to go."

"Lucky cow!" Is the last thing I hear as I cut the call. Yes, she's right, I am lucky and now my mind is made up. I just hope Leo is still up for it.

CHAPTER 20

a s I exit the little office, I'm aware the party is still in full swing as I hear raucous laughter and the sound of Alice singing. Smiling to myself, I beat down any reservations I have and turn towards the stairs. Before I reach them, Rebecca heads outside with Jasper and I smile.

"Hey, you look as if you have your hands full there."

She nods and I see the weariness in her eyes as she moves to the door.

"I'm just taking him outside for a bit. I think the excitement's got to him and he may need a wee."

I don't know why, but she looks so dejected my heart aches for her and despite my raging libido, I say gently, "Would you like some company?"

She shrugs and raises a small smile. "Sure, if you like."

We pull on the ever-present padded coats and head outside in the still of the night. As she sets the little dog down, she looks up at the stars and says in a sad voice, "Do you think my mother can see the same stars where she is?"

"Where is she?"

"I'm not sure." She shrugs. "Somewhere in the Mediterranean on a cruise ship."

"Then yes, probably."

Rebecca nods and pushes her hands in her pockets and looks at me with the tears sparkling like stars in her eyes. "I miss her."

My breath catches and I reach out and touch her arm in sympathy. "What happened?"

"Nothing really. Dad and mum split up years ago, and I have been pushed between them ever since. Phoebe's ok, I guess, but she's not my mum and then when they had Jamie, I felt, well, in the way really."

Shaking her head, she hunches her shoulders and blinks away the tears. "I feel as if I don't fit in anywhere. Mum has a new life now, sailing around the world as an entertainer on the cruise ships. I see her when she's home, but that's less and less these days. Dad tries to include me in his new family, but I don't have much in common with them. I go to university, which is a relief, but I still have to come home for the holidays and always feel a little in the way. Don't get me wrong, they try to make it good for me, but it's forced. It's as if they tread on eggshells around me and I'm just a stranger who visits most of the time."

My heart breaks for her and I say with sympathy, "It must be hard."

Nodding, she smiles as Jasper runs up, wagging his tail. and she reaches down and lifts him up, burying her face in his soft, wet fur.

"Christmas is the worse though. I always loved it when I was little. They made it magical, and I loved everything about it. The shows we went to see, Christmas shopping and the carol concerts and school play. I was so excited to see what Santa brought for me and I couldn't get enough of it. The house was always full of people and my parents entertained - a lot. Although I was an only child, we had many friends, and they always came and filled the house with laughter and good memories. Now Christmas is just another day where I long for it to pass and allow me to get on with living my life on a lonely path. Maybe one day it will get better. Do you think it will?"

I shiver as the icy wind dances through the cracks in my padded coat and try to smile brightly. "Of course it will. It's always a strange time when you move on from childhood and see the season minus the magic. However, as adults, you learn to look for the magic in other ways. Christmas isn't all about Santa and the gifts he brings. It's about spending time with friends and family and appreciating them in your life. There are still shows to go to and parties to attend. The magic of Christmas is in the kindest gesture, like the one when you placed Jasper on Jamie's lap. The joy in his eyes was something money could never buy. There is magic when you spend time with your father and his new family because, ultimately, they will always be in your life. Jamie will always be your brother and you will make happy memories together that you will look back on when you're older with your own families. I know it's difficult now and we all drift in our own way until we find that special someone who we want to build a life with. Then you will find the magic returns as you re-live all your traditions again with your own family and who knows, make some new ones too."

Rebecca smiles warmly and once again, it strikes me just how pretty she is. Her face totally transforms when she loses the sullen look of a teenager in torment and then Jasper barks, a sweet little bark that reminds us that's he's still a puppy.

Crouching down, I pick him up and fondle his soft, sweet ears and he licks my wrist because that's the only bare part of me. Laughing, I nod towards the house. "Maybe we should go back inside and join the rest. It's bitter out here and I don't know about you but I'm freezing."

As we head back, Rebecca says in a small voice, "Thank you, Scarlett. It was good to chat."

I say nothing as she takes Jasper and heads back to the party, leaving me to face my own demons waiting for me upstairs.

Taking a deep breath, I head back towards Leo's room because there's some unfinished business waiting inside.

My heart thumps madly as I reach his door and wonder if he'll be angry with me. Tentatively, I knock on the door and it's not long before it swings open and Leo looks at me with what appears to be relief. "Thank God, Scarlett, are you ok?"

I smile apologetically. "Please, may I come in?"

"Of course." He holds the door open and I step inside, unsure about what I'm about to say.

I feel a little awkward and then, to my surprise, my words all come out in a rush.

"I'm sorry, Leo. I read your book, I mean chapter. I know I shouldn't but it was there, and I was curious and well, I've never been one to resist temptation and well, anyway, I panicked."

He shakes his head. "Panicked, I wouldn't have minded."

"No, I mean, thank you, but no, that's not what I panicked about."

I see the realisation dawn in his eyes and he looks unsure as I blurt out, "I freaked out a bit because the um... person in your book reminded me of... um... well... me, actually. I don't know what I thought and wondered if you had plans to live the action out in reality and, well, I'm not that kind of girl. Actually, I've never been that kind of girl and I just want you to know that I don't do things like this - ever. In fact, I probably won't live up to your expectations and, quite frankly, I wouldn't know how. So, you see, Leo, the trouble is, I may as well be a virgin for all the action I've had. I wanted to, don't get me wrong, of course, I did, but it's not me, well it is me because I wanted it, but it's not me, if you know what I mean. Anyway, to cut a long story short, I took advice and now I'm back to um… carry on where we left off because even though I'm not that sort of girl, I um… well, I would like to be – with you that is, not with a stranger, good god no…"

Suddenly, Leo's lips are on mine, cutting off the pointless words that are spilling from my mouth and he kisses me deep, long and lingering and my knees almost give way. Then he pulls back and whispers, "Stop talking, Scarlett. I'm not about to pounce on you and re-enact my depraved imagination."

"You're not?" Even I hear the disappointment in my voice as he laughs softly. "Not tonight, anyway. No, you were right to cool things down and I think we need to have a conversation before we take this further."

A conversation? Feeling strangely disappointed, I wonder if he wants to iron out some kind of contract before we go any further. It certainly feels like that as he pulls me down beside him on the bed and holds my hand before laughing softly. "You took advice – from whom?"

Feeling my cheeks grow a little warmer, I say softly, "Rita Fairbrother."

I giggle at the look of confusion on his face. "My best friend. I managed to use the office phone and ask for her advice. As it happened, she told me to go for it and what was I waiting for?"

Leo laughs softly and I smile. "She also told me that Gregory had met somebody else."

He looks at me with sympathy, and I shrug. "I'm glad, really. It was over between us and we both needed to move on. The thing is…"

I turn to him and smile. "It means I'm a free agent now. I am single and ready and willing to mingle and, well, you know how it goes. I'm on the market, looking for love, flying solo, an independent woman..."

He laughs and places his finger on my lips as I flush with embarrassment and he smiles sweetly. "Scarlett Robins, allow me to introduce myself. I'm Leo Bradshaw and I'm very pleased to meet you."

"It's nice to meet you, Leo. Do you come here often?"

I giggle as he rolls his eyes and laughs. "You're right, you are new to this."

He stands and heads towards his phone and I watch as he presses a few buttons and then the sound of a romantic Christmas song fills the room. He reaches for my hand and pulls me up, saying, "May I have the pleasure?"

I half curtsey and as he takes me in his arms, I feel as if my heart will burst. As we dance around Leo's room to the sound of White Christmas, I feel just like Rosemary Clooney as I dance in his arms. This feels special, he feels special and I'm so happy I came back.

I'm not sure how long we dance for, but it's well into the night. Occasionally we share a kiss and that's all. Sweet, innocent, old-fashioned courting as they used to say and none of the uncertainty of earlier. In fact, I have never been more certain of anything in my life. I am falling in love with Leo Bradshaw and there's nothing I can do about it.

CHAPTER 21

The sun rises, casting the room in a warm, pink glow and I sigh with contentment. Leo stirs beside me and I sneak a look at perfection; the man who held me in his arms until I fell asleep. We are still fully clothed and just lying on the top of his bed, but last night Leo and I reached an understanding. We both want to take this further but are not going to rush it. If it happens, it will be the most natural thing in the world and not because we can't hold our alcohol.

He stirs and opens his eyes and I say in a whisper, "Morning."

Blinking, he smiles and says huskily, "I could get used to this."

"What?"

"Waking up with you."

I feel a touch embarrassed and he grins. "You are so sweet, Scarlett. Such innocence that's unusual these days. It's kind of refreshing."

I'm not sure whether this is a compliment or not and I laugh awkwardly, "So, what do we do now?"

Leo props himself up on one elbow and grins. "I don't

know about you, but I'm starving. I think we should grab some breakfast and then maybe check out Brenda's gift making course."

I stare at him in surprise. "I wouldn't have thought that was your thing."

He shrugs and sits up, stretching with a sigh of contentment. "It's not, but I wouldn't miss seeing her in action for the world. That woman's a living miracle."

I have to agree with him. "You're not wrong. It will be interesting to hear some more of her stories. It certainly beats the television we're missing."

I head back to my room to change and freshen up and wonder if anybody sees me. It will be all around the hotel in no time that I've made the walk of shame after what will be considered a night of passion in Leo's room. However, I see nobody and part of me feels a little disappointed.

Maybe it's because I have never been that woman. I certainly want to be, you know, the girl who lives life on the edge and couldn't care less what other people think. After last night I'm officially a new woman, free to become the person I always wanted to be, so as I shower and change, I take extra care with my appearance and change it up a little. I brush my long, dark hair and tie it in a messy bun on the top of my head. I've always hated my green eyes, but I accentuate them with some eyeshadow and draw a fine line of kohl along my lids to give them definition. My lipstick choice is scarlet, as my name suggests, and I pull on some tight-fitting jeans and a tight t-shirt, with a small fleece-lined hoodie to keep me warm.

I feel quite pleased with the results and even manage to spray some of my favourite perfume onto the pulse points on my wrists and neck and as I look in the mirror, I don't recognise the woman staring back at me.

This woman looks poised, sophisticated and sure of what

she wants. This woman is charming, good company and keen to chat with strangers. This woman is actually quite pretty when she tries to be and this woman is never looking back because the new Scarlett Robins, as Rita once said, is invincible.

Harold wolf whistles as I pass his room and I laugh softly. Their door is open and I can see Harold tying his shoelaces as Alice brushes her hair while looking in the mirror. She calls out, "Good morning, dear and what a lovely one it is."

I return the greeting and as I venture down the impressive staircase, I hear the sound of Jasper barking and the excited laughter of Jamie as they play together in the hall. I almost trip over a ball they are playing with and Jamie says adorably, "I'm sorry, miss."

Bending down, I retrieve the ball and hold it out to him, smiling warmly. "Call me Scarlett. Here. This is yours, I believe."

He grins and takes the ball from my hands and throws it at the excitable puppy. As he watches Jasper bound and skid down the polished, tiled hallway, Jamie says with a worried voice, "Do you think Santa will know that I'm here?"

I laugh and nod, as if I know all the answers to Santa's secrets. "Of course, he will, and do you know how I know?"

Jamie's eyes widen and he shakes his head solemnly. "How?"

"Because Santa is magic. He knows what every child is doing all the time and adapts his schedule accordingly. You know, it's how he can tell if a child has been naughty or good."

Jamie looks uncomfortable. "What if someone was naughty, don't they get any presents?"

Suddenly, I feel a little apprehensive because I'm not sure if Jamie's parents brought him many gifts, if any and I start to backtrack because the last thing I want is Jamie to think he's been put on the naughty list if there aren't any presents from Santa for him.

"Well, Jamie. It's like this, you see." Frantically, I try to think of a reason why Santa wouldn't come and then we hear a deep, "I wouldn't worry, Jamie. Santa won't forget you because as Scarlett said, he's magic."

I look up and see Ryan smiling at us from the doorway and I blink as I see the huge box of wrapping and ribbons he's holding. Jamie's eyes light up as he sees the impressive bundle of brightly wrapped paper and Ryan winks. "Brenda ordered lots of lovely gift wrapping for her gift making lesson. Would you like to give me a hand, Jamie?"

Jamie calls, "Jasper, come on, we've got work to do."

I watch with amusement as Ryan heads off with the two of them in tow, looking like the pied piper. Breathing a sigh of relief, I see Marigold heading out from the kitchen, and she looks relieved when she sees me. "Oh good, Scarlett. I don't suppose you could lend a hand with breakfast? It's busy with all the extra guests and I'm trying to juggle my tomatoes with my fried eggs in there."

Glad of something to do, I follow her into the kitchen, feeling quite positive about it all.

By the time we've served everyone breakfast, I manage to grab some myself and sigh with relief as I finally sit down opposite Leo.

He laughs and pours me some tea. "It's exhausting running a hotel, isn't it?"

I nod and accept the tea gratefully. "It sure is. No wonder Mr and Mrs Scott needed to go on a cruise. It's a shame though."

"What is?"

"This place." I wave my hand around and feel my heart

sink. "Look at it, Leo. It's such an amazing place and I hate to think of it being bulldozed to make way for progress. Do you think there's anything we can do to find out what's happening?"

He looks at me thoughtfully. "It's tricky because we don't have any internet or phone signal."

"But we do. Remember I used the phone last night to call my friend."

Leo smiles. "Of course, maybe we could use that to find out who bought Holly Island and then go from there."

Feeling a little brighter, I feel quite excited. Maybe we can discover who the developer is and find out their plans. It would be lovely if they intend on keeping the place as it is with just a bit of updating.

Leo looks at me with a thoughtful expression. "What are you thinking?"

"That I wish we could always come here. I don't know about you, but I'm missing it already and I haven't even left yet. What if we can't ever come back? That would be unbearable."

Leo nods and takes a sip of his orange juice, looking thoughtful. "What are you going to do when you leave, Scarlett?"

His question takes me by surprise, probably because I haven't even thought of it myself. I feel unsure and he is looking at me with such intensity I feel a little pressured and just shrug. "I haven't thought about it. I suppose I stopped thinking when I left home and came here. It was just important that I did, don't ask me why. Now, faced with the prospect of going home, I'm not sure what I'll do. That's bad, isn't it?"

He nods. "Some may say it is but not me."

"Why not?"

"Because I'm much the same. I was supposed to be home

by now and declaring my love for Davina. It was all worked out, and I was about to spend Christmas congratulating myself on how lucky I was. My job probably hinges on that decision and as my flat comes with that job, I may have also made myself homeless."

"Surely not, I mean, they may be disappointed, but they're still your family. They wouldn't throw you out on the streets."

"Maybe you're right. Family should count for something, I suppose. Anyway, it doesn't really matter because I'm quitting my job, anyway."

I stare at him in shock. "When did you decide that?"

"Last night."

I feel a little responsible although I don't know why and say quickly, "Are you sure you're not being a little hasty."

He shakes his head and sighs. "Not at all. I earn enough from my books to make my own way, so I'm listening to my heart and setting up on my own."

Feeling a little uncomfortable, I say hesitantly, "Um… your books, you say you've published some before this one. I've never seen them in our bookshop. Where do you sell them?"

"Online." He laughs. "You'd be amazed at how many books never make the shelves of bookshops around the world. For instance, the books I write will never win any literary prizes. They will never be under discussion in your average book club and they will certainly never be on Richard and Judy's book club list. But I do have a following and they like what I do, so that's enough for me. I don't want to be the next J K Rowling, although I wouldn't turn it down if it came my way. I just want to make a living and be free to do whatever I want. If I want to lock myself away in places such as this, I want the freedom to do it. If I want to go on holiday for three months, I don't want to have to ask anyone's permission. I just need enough money to make my life comfortable and I will be happy with that."

"That sounds like Utopia."

Leaning across the table, he reaches for my hand and entwines my fingers with his. "It will be if you come with me."

CHAPTER 22

*H*is words hit me like a bolt out of the blue and I just stare at him in total surprise. When I find my voice, it's only to say, "Me?"

He raises my hand to his lips and kisses it softly, and his eyes sparkle with excitement as he smiles. "Yes. I want to leave Holly Island with you, Scarlett, because I have a good feeling about us."

"Us?"

"I told you that I knew you were the one as soon as you arrived, and that feeling has never left me. We can take things as slowly as you like because I intend to make you the happiest woman alive. So, what do you say, leave Holly Island with me after Christmas and pick a place you want to go? It can be anywhere in the world and I'll make it happen. Let's have an adventure, Scarlett, and do it together."

My heart beats so quickly I'm in danger of passing out. This is so unexpected, so strange and so amazing. I almost can't think straight.

He is looking at me with such an expression of hope mixed with excitement it's contagious and I find myself caught up in it all and say quickly, "Yes, I can't believe I'm saying this but... yes."

A wide smile breaks out across his face and he reaches over and grasps my hand firmly, squeezing it hard, saying. "That's fantastic. You won't regret it; I'll make sure of that. Now, all we have to do is find out where we want to go and then our adventure can begin."

"What adventure?"

We look up and see Martin walking past looking curious, and Leo smiles happily. "Scarlett and I are leaving Holly Island together and are jetting off anywhere she chooses. It will be amazing."

Martin whistles slowly, "Wow, I've got to hand it to you, you don't hang around. It makes me feel quite jealous."

We look in surprise as he takes a seat and then says in a low voice, "Listen, I've been meaning to ask but there's never the right time."

We look at him expectantly and he smiles. "You know Fiona and I are renewing our vows on Christmas Eve, well... we were thinking, actually hoping, that you would both act as our witnesses, you know, a sort of best man and brides-maid, if they even have them at vow renewals."

Leo nods and slaps him on the back like most men seem to do and says happily, "Of course, I will, I'd be honoured."

They look at me and I feel a little uncomfortable because what if Fiona doesn't want me tagging along? It's difficult though so I just nod and say gratefully, "I would love to, if you're sure it's what Fiona wants."

Martin grins and calls across the dining room, "Fiona, I've asked Leo and Scarlett to be our witnesses and they said yes."

I watch as a broad smile breaks across Fiona's face as she rushes to join us and I feel settled by the obvious happiness in her eyes. "That's great. You don't mind, do you, Scarlett? I mean, it won't be a burden or anything, will it?"

"Of course not, I would love to be part of your special day."

Martin smiles sweetly at her, taking her hand in his. "You know, I couldn't love Fiona any more than I do, even more than the first time we got married. Christmas Eve can't come soon enough because this time it will be different."

Fiona turns a little pink as Martin gazes at her lovingly. I catch Leo's eye and he looks a little uncomfortable, so I say quickly, "What do you need us to do?"

Martin tears his eyes away from his wife and shrugs. "I'm not sure, really. I mean, we have rings and you don't have to give a speech or anything. I suppose just be there throughout the ceremony and act as our official witnesses."

Fiona says nervously, "Any word on the vicar?"

Martin looks at her reassuringly. "No, but I'm sure he won't let us down. Now, we need to head across to Brenda and see if she'll be our official organiser. I'm sure she'll relish the role and then we must ask Rebecca and Jamie to be bridesmaid and page boy. I hope they agree. It will be good to include them."

They make their excuses and leave to find Brenda, and Leo shakes his head. "Well, this is a morning for surprises."

As I watch the couple leave, I say in a low voice, "It must be hard for them."

"Why?"

"Well, after finding them… um… well… you know. Martin must be very tolerant after what happened with his brother."

Leo frowns. "I'm not sure I would be as forgiving in his shoes. It's the ultimate betrayal."

I agree with him, which makes me think that Martin must have been a saint in a former life because it's obvious he adores Fiona and you would never believe they had problems.

Leo smiles. "Come on, let's go and see if we can use the phone."

"Why?" I have completely forgotten our earlier conversation, and Leo raises his eyes. "We want to find out what's in store for Holly Island – remember? I don't know about you, but the curiosity has got the better of me and for my own peace of mind, I'd like to know. I'm going to call my secretary and ask her to do some digging on our behalf."

We head to the office and I share his curiosity. Holly Island is such a magical place. It would be a shame for it to change, although I wouldn't complain if it stayed as a hotel.

Luckily, the office is empty and I nod towards the phone resting on the battered oak desk, that's covered in various piles of papers and files. Leo grabs hold of it and frowns. "What?"

"There's no dialling tone."

He presses it again and then says with disappointment, "Nothing. Was it this phone you used?"

I nod and reach for the handset. "Yes, definitely."

As I try my luck, I also come up blank and Leo shrugs. "It must have gone again. You were probably lucky and hit it at the right time. Never mind, we'll try later. It's probably gift making time, anyway."

We head off to the lounge and I don't think anything more about the phone. Power comes and goes on Holly Island regardless of the weather and it appears that the connections are always on very shaky ground.

CHAPTER 23

*B*renda beams around the room, "Well, I must say this is a fantastic turnout."

She looks down at her clipboard. "Right then. I have some different activities that you can attend based on your own preferences. Firstly, there is a food gift class courtesy of Marigold in the kitchen. She will help you make sweets, biscuits and other tempting treats that you can box up and place under the Christmas tree for your chosen recipient. Then I have an Art Class in the library, courtesy of Phoebe, who has kindly agreed to supervise anyone who wants to make Christmas cards or pictures for the ones they love. Then I have a decoration making class outdoors with Fiona, who is apparently a dab hand at twisting twigs into various shapes and is also excellent at making wreaths and foliage decorations."

She looks down at the board and says, "Oh yes, um... Harold has kindly offered to demonstrate his knowledge of making flavoured gins and that will take place in the bar, for obvious reasons. Oh, and Alice has volunteered to help with packaging and gift wrapping. Is there any other skill anyone wants to add?"

Rebecca speaks up to my surprise and says shyly, "I can show people how to make beauty products from household items."

Brenda beams at her. "Wonderful darling."

She turns to Colin and says briskly, "Colin, you are responsible for making sure everyone has what they need. It will be just like the time we helped organise the Harrods special pre-Christmas gala evening. You remember, the one where they opened up in the evening for the local celebrities and VIPs who didn't want to shop with the riff-raff. Goodness, what an evening that was. We had to make sure everyone knew their place and had everything they needed and do you remember that Saudi Prince was quite enamoured of me?"

She laughs shrilly and lowers her voice, talking behind her hand so that Colin can't see what the rest of us can. "It was touch and go there for a minute whether I'd join his harem. Goodness, imagine the life I would have had."

Alice looks at her with wide eyes and giggles. "I would have bitten his hand off. Goodness, imagine that, the plaything of a prince. What stopped you, Brenda?"

Brenda giggles, which is totally unlike her, and throws a quick glance at Colin before saying conspiratorially, "I doubt there's a man alive who could beat Colin in that department. Let's just say, his crown jewels are far more valuable than all the money in the world."

We all stare at Colin, who grins and I stifle a giggle, Colin! Wow, who knew?

We split up according to our preferences. Leo decides to join the gin-making class, while I decide on the wreath making and twisted twigs with Fiona.

My group grabs our winter coats, hats and gloves and

head outside. The group consists of Fiona, Jamie and Martin and as the cool breeze hits us, I question my sanity as I picture the warm kitchen which any sane person would surely have gravitated towards.

We head down to the woods where Fiona assures us that she'll find everything we need and I laugh as I see Jasper trailing Jamie through the trees. We are instructed to look for twigs while she will cut the necessary foliage needed for wreath making.

As we work, I find myself chatting to Martin about his impending ceremony.

"It's a shame the hotel wasn't staffed, Martin. You must have paid a lot for the whole vow renewal experience. Tell me what you were supposed to get."

He shrugs and doesn't look overly upset. "We booked the honeymoon suite that was to be stocked with champagne and red roses. I had asked for chocolates to be delivered and a candlelit dinner for two in our room on the night of our arrival. They had promised us both a couple's massage although now we're here, I'm not sure how that would have worked because they haven't got any kind of spa or beauty room to speak of."

He says sadly, "I wanted everything to be perfect. They were arranging the whole thing. The flower decorations that were going to decorate the room set aside for the ceremony if it was too cold to have it outside. There was to be live classical music as Fiona walked down the aisle and a special cake and dinner to celebrate afterwards. I ordered pink champagne and for fireworks to be set off that evening. It was to be a magical experience and now we'll just have to try to recreate it ourselves."

I feel sorry for them and say enthusiastically, "I'm sure we could all manage to make that happen. Maybe not the fireworks, but I could help Marigold in the kitchen and I'm sure

Phoebe would do the decorating. We could make it special for you both, I'm sure of it."

Martin looks so grateful; I feel glad I offered. Then he lowers his voice and says sadly, "The trouble is, I wish Fiona would forget the past. It's weighing her down, the guilt, that is. I keep on telling her it doesn't matter, but she doesn't believe me. To be honest, I'm not sure what to do to put her mind at ease."

"You know, Martin, I think you're a very special person to feel bad for her after what you've been through. It must have been a shock and any lesser man wouldn't have been as forgiving."

He smiles sadly. "The trouble is, Scarlett, what Fiona did was inevitable."

I stare at him in shock and he nods. "You see, women are like flowers. They are all unique, requiring different types of care. There are some who require little or no water to survive. They thrive on little or no attention and stand proud and magnificent despite it. Others need a lot of care and coaxing to survive at all. Some need constant attention and care to bring them to full bloom. Fiona is that flower, Scarlett. She needs reassurance and to feel desired and loved. I never gave it to her, so I only have myself to blame. I wasn't the caring husband that I am now. I was obsessed with making money and providing the material things I thought we both deserved. I completely lost sight of the fact that the most precious thing I had was her and hardly gave her a second thought as I went out to work each day. I worked long and hard and yes, we reaped the financial rewards. However, Fiona isn't the exotic beauty that thrives on what it gets from the atmosphere. She has deep roots that need constant feeding, and that's where I failed. My brother saw his chance and gave her what I did not. It was understandable what happened and I don't blame her at all for it."

I stare at him with newfound respect, and he smiles ruefully. "My brother and I were always competitive. What you don't know is that he was engaged to be married to Fiona in the first place."

He laughs at my shocked expression. "Yes, when I first met her, she was introduced to me as his girlfriend. I couldn't believe that my brother had managed to convince a woman as beautiful as she was and still is, to go out with him. You see, Scarlett, Fiona is beautiful inside and out and I'm ashamed to admit I set out to take her from my own brother."

I feel fascinated by the words that spill from his lips and even the sound of Fiona calling us doesn't distract my attention as he says quickly, "So, you see, if anyone is the bad guy in all this, it's me. I made up some tale about my brother cheating on her and she believed every word. To this day she doesn't know I made it up, which is why I can forgive her indiscretion. No, I always wanted Fiona and I make sure I always get what I want. So, you see, I win again because now she will do everything she can to make me happy because of her own guilty conscience. I will make her happy for the rest of her life and my brother loses – again."

Fiona comes through the trees and looks a little cross. "There you are, didn't you hear me calling you? I need some help to gather up the foliage."

Martin winks as he heads towards her and I hear him saying, "I'm sorry, darling, I got chatting, you know what I'm like. Now, I'm all yours. What do you want me to do?"

I watch him place his arm around her shoulders and they head off back into the trees and I stare after them in shock. What did I just hear? That was unexpected.

My opinion of Martin has now changed completely and I feel sorry for Fiona. I wonder what would have happened if she had stayed with his brother? Now all I can think about is that she's been manipulated into a relationship with the wrong brother and may have been happier with the first one.

"Jasper."

My attention is brought back to the present as I hear the worry in Jamie's voice. Quickly, I head towards it and see Jamie looking around him frantically. "I can't find Jasper."

He looks close to tears and I say in a calm voice. "He can't have gone far; I'll help you look."

We set off through the trees calling Jasper's name and I soon forget what I just heard as something much more important claims my attention.

CHAPTER 24

*W*e call and call for the little puppy and as I see Jamie's frantic little face, my heart lurches. The wind whistles through the trees and I almost can't feel my toes as we try desperately to find the little puppy. "Jasper!!!"

We walk further and further into the forest and I'm suddenly aware that we have lost sight of where we are. Crouching down, I say in a firm, decisive voice, "Listen, we need to head back the way we came; he may have doubled back. If he hasn't, then we can gather the others to come and help search for him before it gets dark."

I smile, trying to appear unconcerned. "I'm sure he's back at the hotel wondering where you are right now."

Jamie's bottom lip trembles and his eyes are worried as he says in a small voice, "What if we don't find him? It will be all my fault."

"Of course, it isn't." I shake my head and stand up. "Come on, let's head back and keep calling him. I'm guessing he isn't far. After all, he can't go anywhere. This place is an island, remember."

I try not to think of the cliffs that hug the island. I try not to imagine the cold, unforgiving sea that whips the shoreline and I try not to think of the many pitfalls that could be waiting for an inexperienced little dog.

Instead, I call for the puppy along with Jamie and try to believe that he's right where I said he was.

After a while, Jamie says in a small voice, "If we don't find him, will Santa put me on the naughty list for not taking good care of him?"

Oh no, not this again. I say lightly, "Jamie, you don't have to worry about being put on the naughty list. Why would Santa even think you weren't anything less than a kind, helpful little boy?"

He looks nervous. "Because I wet the bed."

"Oh, every child does that. It's normal and if Santa held that against you, he would be out of a job."

He nods, but still looks worried. "Scarlett?"

"Yes, Jamie."

"Are secrets bad?"

"What do you mean?"

He shrugs. "I found out a secret and was told that if I tell anyone Santa won't come."

My heart starts hammering inside me and I say gently, "You don't need to worry about Santa, Jamie. He'll come regardless. Anyway, who told you that?"

I hold my breath as he looks worried. "Rebecca."

"Listen, I'm sure your parents wouldn't want you keeping any secrets from them. Maybe Rebecca was playing with you, you know that's what sisters do, tease their little brothers. When did you discover this secret, anyway?"

He doesn't answer because suddenly, a small, furry, bundle, races towards us barking excitedly and Jamie shouts, "Jasper, I knew you'd come back."

The relief is enormous as I laugh at the sight of the little boy holding the wriggling puppy in his arms. What a relief.

However, as we walk back to the hotel, I bring way more with me than just a handful of twigs. It's the weight of responsibility because in these woods I have been told two things I would rather not know and I'm not sure what on earth to do about either of them?

We soon reach the hotel and Jamie races off with Jasper and I'm guided to the lounge where a table has been set up for us to make our creations. We are joined by Alice and Brenda and spend a lovely afternoon learning how to decorate a twisted wreath and how to make twig hearts with just a ball of twine and a festive ribbon.

However, as I watch Fiona laughing at something Martin whispers in her ear, I feel uncomfortable. I just can't get what he told me out of my mind. I wonder what Fiona would do if she ever found out he lied to her. Would she regret leaving his brother for him and what about his brother? He must have strong feelings for her to have tried to steal her back again. Goodness, torn between two brothers, even Leo couldn't make this one up.

Alice leans across and whispers, "You know dear, I'm having such a lovely time here, are you?"

I nod, feeling a little distracted by my thoughts and as she holds up a little willow heart proudly, she says in a whisper, "I'm going to give this to Harold."

I smile, "That's a lovely idea. I'm sure he'll be happy and it will always remind him of you and your amazing time here."

She giggles and then lowers her voice still further. "Between me and you dear, I've got designs on Harold."

I stare at her in surprise, "But I thought you were a free agent and heading off with another man to celebrate the new year?"

Shaking her head, Alice says firmly, "No, Harold is the man for me and I want him to realise that. You know, when you get to our age dear, you don't have long left. Every minute is precious which is why I didn't sit around moping after Fred died. I realised that my life is now on fast forward and I'm struggling to keep up. It's my hips, you know. They've taken quite a pounding lately and well, I would like to give them a rest if I can."

Feeling quite ill at the thought of Alice's hips taking a pounding, I say weakly, "So, what's your plan?"

Shrugging, she ties a bow to her heart twig with a flourish. "I haven't worked it out yet but when I leave Holly Island, I want it to be with Harold by my side for the rest of our lives."

She starts to hum as she tidies up her work station and I feel bad. Thinking about the length of time either of them may have left fills me with a sadness that I can't explain. It must be hard to have so much life left in you knowing it may end sooner than you're ready for. Maybe she is right and you should live every day as if it's your last. I could learn a lot from Alice and after the day I've had, I think I need to have a lie-down.

Why is it that everyone around me is holding a secret they think I should know about? Why can't I be left in blissful ignorance to bathe in the warm glow of my own good luck? Now all I have is a shed load of anxiety as I see the faces all around me. Martin, Fiona and Jamie. Rebecca and the secret she's keeping and Leo working out a way to be free from his arrangement. Then there's Gregory waiting at home with another woman not knowing I know. He must feel as guilty as I do and worrying about my imminent return and having to break the devastating news that we don't have a future. Why is life so complicated?

I look up as Leo heads into the room looking a little flushed and stinking of gin. He slumps down beside me and grins. "Brilliant afternoon. I must say, I've discovered a new love of making things from scratch. Just wait until you see what I've made for you."

He winks and I smile weakly as I twist the little heart around in my hands. Christmas seems so near and yet so far because between now and Christmas day, I have a feeling that everything could go badly wrong.

CHAPTER 25

The rest of the day is spent alternating between classes and I can't remember when I last had so much fun.

My favourite is with Phoebe in the Art class and I look with wonder at the picture she is drawing of Jasper. She smiles as I gush over it and says a little sadly. "I'm not sure what to do when we leave Holly Island."

"What do you mean?"

She sighs and sets her pencil down. "This – Jasper. Jamie's fallen in love with him and it's an impossible situation. You see, if it were up to me, I'd give him a home, but it's not."

"Who is it up to then?"

Phoebe smiles sadly. "Kevin. He always said no pets or animals because they are too expensive and a tie we can live without. I would love to let Jamie have just one little friend to care for, but Kevin is adamant."

"Maybe he's changed his mind now. I mean, it's obvious how much Jamie loves Jasper and he is such a sweet little dog who couldn't love him?"

She looks thoughtful. "You know, I may just ask him

again. Who knows, the spirit of Christmas and Harold's gin may make him change his mind?"

Nodding, I lean back and look at my own creation. I've drawn a picture of Holly Island for Leo, but it's nowhere near as good as Phoebe's. Art was never my forte, but I suppose it's the thought that counts.

Sighing at my own inadequacies, I smile. "It doesn't hurt to ask, I suppose."

She looks across at my picture and nods with approval. "It's good, Scarlett."

Then I watch as the light dims in her eyes and she says in a sad voice, "You know, it's been a difficult year. We thought coming here would help heal a rift that is growing between us and showing signs of getting wider, not smaller."

"Rebecca?"

Looking surprised, she nods. "How did you guess?"

"She told me a little of her story when I met her outside last night. It must be hard trying to care for another woman's daughter, especially when she resents you."

I see the shock in Phoebe's eyes and say quickly, "Not that she said she did. In fact, she said you were nice."

"What else did she say?" Phoebe looks a little worried, and I try to put her mind at rest.

"Just that she finds it hard fitting in. She feels a little out of the loop and as if she's in the way with her father's new family."

Phoebe looks as if she's going to cry and I feel bad. "I think it's normal, though. It's a difficult situation for everyone and must be hard."

"It is. I mean, I suppose I try a little too hard if I'm honest and it probably comes across as false. The thing is though, Harriet, Rebecca's mother is quite a free spirit. She always has been and certainly isn't a candidate for the mother of the year. Don't get me wrong, she absolutely adores Rebecca, but she loves her freedom just as much. The cruise ship was a spur-of-the-moment whim, and she was packed and depositing Rebecca on our doorstop quicker than the ink dried on her contract. She's away for nine months of the year and although she keeps in regular contact, it's just not enough for a vulnerable girl."

She looks so concerned I feel bad for her, and she sighs. "I try to be a friend to her, but she's so angry most of the time. I know it's not aimed at me, but she must resent me in her mother's place and when Jamie came along, she felt even more pushed out. I know she loves him, but he also irritates her as little brothers have a tendency to do. It's fine because she's away at Uni for most of the time, but then it only high-lights the problem when she comes home because she feels excluded and as if she doesn't fit in."

I see their problem and don't really know what I can say to make it seem better. Then I remember the secret she's making Jamie keep and feel a little bad. Maybe it's nothing and just a gift she's bought for her father. In fact, I'm going to think it is because I'm getting a headache just thinking about it.

We are interrupted by Brenda, who heads towards us looking pleased with herself. "You know that daughter of yours is a hidden gem."

Phoebe looks surprised as Brenda nods emphatically. "The things that girl can do with an egg white and a bowl of oatmeal – pure genius, if you ask me. She's wasted at univer-sity and should be developing her own skincare line. In fact, it reminds me of when I was headhunted by Elizabeth Arden. They were keen for me to head up their European division and develop a new youth serum. Well, I was flattered and everything but I was too busy running for local office at the time. Never mind, I always wonder where I'd be now if I'd taken them up on their offer, instead of becoming the chair-woman at the local women's institute."

She wanders off and Phoebe shakes her head slowly. "You know, I still can't make up my mind whether she's making all that stuff up."

I laugh as we hear Brenda shouting, "Hurry up if you want to make chocolate fudge before dinner."

Phoebe laughs. "Next, she'll be telling us she won the last series of Bake Off. Goodness, I feel quite inadequate."

She stands and takes one last look at her picture before saying brightly, "Anyway, I had better check on Kevin, God only knows how much gin he's had already and as for Jamie, I haven't seen him for hours, some mother I am."

I watch her walk away and feel bad for her. She just wants everyone to be happy, and it's obvious they aren't. Maybe this trip will help them bond more as a family. I'd like to think so because I believe in the magic of Holly Island and Christmas and hope that sometimes miracles do happen.

The day turns to a dusky evening and I welcome the sight of the fire dancing in the grate. Leo comes to find me and we spend a delicious hour curled up on the settee with mugs of hot chocolate and tales of a day well spent.

Luckily, Phoebe volunteered to help Marigold with dinner and I find my eyes closing as the heat of the fire causes my limbs to relax and the fatigue overpowers me as Leo rubs my shoulder gently.

As I drift off to sleep, I thank God that I found him. Christmas miracles do exist, at least in my case.

CHAPTER 26

*A*fter dinner, Leo and I watch a Christmas movie on the DVD and life couldn't get more perfect. However, I feel a little anxious about later and wonder if tonight's the night when our relationship accelerates past the point of no return. I have watched Leo throughout most of the day and every time I see him, I feel a little shiver of expectation run through me. I do want Leo, very much as it happens, but there's still a small doubt in my mind that I just won't shape up.

I feel curious about his writing and tentatively broach the subject as the film finishes. "You know, Leo, maybe we will watch one of your stories made into a movie one day."

He laughs out loud. "I doubt it, and if it was, it probably wouldn't be on mainstream television."

I feel curious and have to ask, "Why do you write... um... x-rated stories, anyway? I'm guessing you could make far more money from writing general fiction. What made you choose, um..."

He grins. "Contemporary romance."

I nod as he laughs. "Because the readers are voracious.

They devour the stories and are keen for the next one. I sell many copies and they still want more. To be honest, Scarlett, I didn't start out wanting to write these stories, but well, I just fell into it. My first one was the age-old tale of tattooed bad boy meets shy, inexperienced, virgin. You know, the usual." I feel my cheeks flame as he grins wickedly. "Then there was the billionaire who was the most eligible bachelor in New York who fell instantly in love with the woman who gave him a parking ticket. Oh, and the nerd who caught the attention of the star quarterback at college who turned his back on his womanising days to declare his eternal love for a girl who collected anime memorabilia. You know the sort of thing."

He grins and I know he's teasing me, so I say firmly, "Then maybe I should read one of these bestsellers and see what I've apparently been missing out on. Obviously, I'm so behind the times I know nothing."

Leo laughs. "Then follow me, my little bookworm, and allow me to enlighten you."

I feel quite nervous as I follow Leo to his room. I hope he didn't mean to show me literally in the non-literary meaning of the word. What if this is it and he is about to demonstrate where he gets his inspiration from? When did I last clean my teeth and did I shave any time soon? Is my underwear clean and I think I forgot to put deodorant on? These and many other more x-rated thoughts spin around my mind until we reach his room and he wrenches the door open and marches inside, saying over his shoulder, "Come on, I've got something for you."

I think I almost faint as I follow him inside and think about closing my eyes rather than see what he wants to show me. Instead, I laugh nervously, "That old story, come to my room and I'll show you my etchings. Honestly, Leo, I had you down as someone more original than that."

His laughter makes me look at him in surprise and he holds out his iPad. "Open the Kindle App and choose your story. They're all on there and you can be my harshest critic."

He holds out the iPad and I reach for it tentatively. To be honest, I can't wait to start reading and say rather dismissively, "Ok, if you insist, but it's not really my kind of thing."

He just smiles and as I take the tablet, he looks at his watch. "You can take it to bed if you like. I've got time to get a few more words down, so you can be left in peace to read while I write."

I feel a little grateful for the space he's offering me and smile with relief. "That sounds great. I'll take it to my room, if you don't mind. At least it gives you time to work and I'm so tired I may just have a bath and then tuck myself in with your book."

Leo smiles and then pulls me into his arms, saying softly, "Sleep well. I've enjoyed today, and I never thought I'd say that."

"Why?"

"Because any gifts I've ever given have been ordered online or sourced by my secretary. If she could see me making things from scratch, she wouldn't believe her eyes. I've enjoyed every minute though, and having Harold as a companion was entertaining. You know, the stories that man tells would make your hair curl."

He leans down and kisses me softly and sighs. "I hate that I've got to work, but my deadline is fast approaching. I'll see you for breakfast though."

I kiss him lightly and wink. "It's a date. Don't stay up too long."

I pull away, gripping the iPad tightly as I leave him to create more stories and feel excited and yet a little apprehensive about what I'm about to read. As the door clicks shut and I start my journey to my room, I hear a giggle and gruff laugh coming from a room on the floor below. Looking over the bannisters, I see Rebecca leaving one of the rooms and looking around furtively. She is smiling at something and I wonder what's going on. She heads back down the hallway towards what must be her own room and for some reason, I hesitate. Then I wish I hadn't because the door opens and I see Harold heading out, pulling on his jacket and looking extremely pleased with himself.

CHAPTER 27

*I*t's all perfectly innocent, nothing to see here, it's just your dirty mind...

I can't help my imagination spiralling out of control as I think about Rebecca and... Harold! I cringe at my own wicked thoughts and bolt to my room, and shut the door with a resounding thump.

No, there will be a perfectly innocent explanation for what I just saw and it must be something to do with her secret. I almost put my head in my hands and groan. Rebecca's secret. Please don't let it be what I very much hope it isn't.

Feeling flustered, I run a hot bath and empty a whole bottle of trial size bubble bath into it. Thankfully, Marigold showed me where they keep the complimentary toiletries and I have been indulging ever since.

The steam from the water does little to cool down my imagination and, as I remove my make-up, I stare in the steamed-up mirror at a distorted expression of horror. In fact, if Leo wrote books like Stephen King, it wouldn't be far removed from the sick tale playing around in my mind.

Splashing some cold water on my face, I remove my clothes and throw them in a heap on the floor and gently lower myself into the hot, sweet-smelling water. As I lean back and reach for Leo's iPad, I try to cleanse my dirty mind as well as my body as I start to read The Billionaire's Hot Ticket to Paradise.

I'm not sure if it's the scorching water or the words that burn on the screen before me, but I start to feel extremely hot. In fact, I start panting because I'm burning up – everywhere!

For some reason though, I can't stop reading and soon one chapter turns to ten chapters as I completely lose myself in decadence.

In fact, I almost forget to breathe as I feel every emotion that plays out on the screen before me. The water starts to cool but the temperature inside me doesn't. I can't seem to get enough as I am pulled into a wicked world of sinful lust and dubious morals. I am that girl in this book as I lust after the enigmatic, super cool, Ethan Trent who runs Voltair Steel. Wow, I am that woman who leans across his windscreen and plasters a penalty ticket on it while her curves mould themselves to the glass. I catch the eye of the billionaire as his eyes sparkle with lust through the glass and my own breath steams up the tablet screen just as Jennifer Ireland's does as she lies across his Lamborghini.

It takes a superhuman effort on my part to drag myself from the now freezing bath and wrap myself in the warm and cosy towel that has been heating on the radiator. I sit on the toilet seat and devour the words before my eyes. I feel the heat travel through my body as the two people get to um… know each other and my imagination runs riot as I picture myself enjoying every delicious pleasure our heroine receives.

The clock ticks on the wall and the sound of laughter

bubbles up from somewhere outside. The hours tick by and I only move to wrap myself in my Minnie Mouse pyjamas and bury myself in the warm and cosy duvet. The only light in the room is the one that shines out from the screen before me and as the hours' tick by, my imagination goes into meltdown.

Four hours later and I lower the tablet to my knees and breathe again. So, that's what passes as romance these days. Goodness, Mr Saracen needs to go on a refresher course on the trends of today. I never knew I would be so engrossed in what used to be known as porn, but now I've read one, like an addict in search of a high, I want more.

However, my eyes won't cooperate and they grow heavy and weak. The feather pillows beneath my head beckon me towards them. The heat from the warm bed wraps me in comfort and, as the feeling of blissful happy endings rocks me to sleep, my dreams are now a very different kind.

I wake in the early hours and it's pitch dark. There isn't a sound to be heard, not even a passing owl. Holly Island has no street lights and the curtains are heavy at the window, blocking out any sliver of moonlight that dares to creep through the cracks. Suddenly, I'm wide awake and desperate and I reach for the iPad eagerly and turn to my next fix.

Settling down, I'm grateful for the few hours of sleep that have given me a renewed energy to devour yet another one of Leo's stories. I read with a hunger I have never experienced before. Maybe because this is so different from anything I have ever read and maybe it's because of the man who wrote them, but I am spellbound by these books. The image he creates with words keeps me turning the pages and as the words dance before my eyes, so do the hopes and dreams they create. Thinking about Leo typing away in his room, living these stories in his mind, I feel myself burning with a need for something I was unsure of until now. In one of these books, the woman would be tiptoeing down the hallway dressed in nothing but a wicked attitude and an overcoat. I wonder what Leo would think if I knocked on his door dressed in my finest underwear, begging for a cup of something warm to take off the chill.

I lie back in disbelief as I feel different inside. I feel like a woman for the first time in my life and now I know the power of words. Leo was right, he's good at this and as I reach the end of another story, my mind is made up. I want to experience the magic of love for myself. I want to be this sensuous woman that controls her life and calls the shots. I want Leo to fall at my feet and worship the ground I stand on because I am sick and tired of being boring Scarlett Robins, the drifter in life who just makes do with whatever life throws at her.

No, Leo has come into my life for a reason and together we are going to travel the world and have adventures, just as soon as Christmas is over and I've broken the news to my parents. Their little girl has grown up and is bolting from the nest in six-inch heels and suspenders after a man who has ruined her for anyone else.

CHAPTER 28

*M*y head feels light, and it feels as if I have sand blocking my eyes. My body feels heavy, and it's difficult to move my limbs. Four hours' sleep does this to a person, but inside I am on fire. I have a new zest for life and I am grabbing this opportunity with both hands.

As I dress, it's with a critical eye. I choose my clothes with care as I try desperately to attract rather than repel. Gone are the warm sweaters and jogging bottoms. Today I feel like a new woman and must dress accordingly. The trouble is, the only thing suitable is my skinny jeans and a tight-fitting white top. Despite how cold I may feel, I brace myself for a bit of discomfort in the name of getting what I want. Because I do want something and I want it bad. Leo.

I take great care with my make-up and brush my hair until it shines. A liberal spray of perfume finishes the look, and I head from my room like a hunter on the prowl. I feel different somehow. It's as if I've been re-born and, like Alice, I don't want to waste a moment of it.

As I descend the stairs, I keep a lookout for Leo. However, the first person I see is Ryan, and he's not alone. I watch with interest as he laughs at something Rebecca says as she hugs Jasper with a huge smile on her face. She looks so different from the sullen teenager that arrived, and I feel happy for her. Ryan looks as if Christmas has arrived early because he stares at her with a look of total adoration and a dart of worry hits me hard. This could spell trouble because he is several years older than her and I try to push aside the memory of a much older one that entertained her in one of the unoccupied rooms last night.

As I approach, they look up and smile and I feel bad for my dirty thoughts.

"Hey, Scarlett, you're looking amazing today."

Ryan smiles and I return it tenfold. "Oh thanks, I just thought I'd dress up a little, after all, it is Christmas."

I giggle stupidly and even I roll my eyes at how silly I sound. Rebecca smiles sweetly and says to Ryan. "Thanks, it's not too much trouble though, is it?"

He switches his attention back to her and the look he gives her demonstrates his desire to walk over hot coals should she ask. She raises her eyes as Jasper struggles and laughs. "I should take him outside. He's been cooped up far too long already."

Ryan nods and says quickly, "I'll walk with you and we can, um…"

He looks at me nervously and then says awkwardly, "Yes, well, um… see you later, Scarlett, enjoy your day."

They head outside and as the icy wind blows in from the doorway, it reminds me that I should really have worn something warmer. As I look down, I almost shriek with horror as I see my assets standing proudly to attention and I scurry into the dining room as quickly as possible, desperate to grab a spot by the fire. This is not how it would play out in Leo's book.

Luckily, my preferred table is free and I'm pleased to see

the breakfast has been laid out already and settle down and watch Alice playing footsie with Harold under the table. She sees me watching and winks, and I laugh to myself. Maybe she reads Leo's books. It would certainly explain a few things.

Fiona and Martin look up and wave and Martin calls out, "Not long now, Scarlett. We're full steam ahead with the preparations and it should be a magical evening."

"I can't wait," I call out as I help myself to hot coffee and a Danish pastry.

As I wait for Leo, my heart starts thumping as I try to think of something witty and clever to say about his book. Maybe I shouldn't admit to staying up for most of the night reading and maybe I should just act impressed but unaffected. It will certainly be strange looking at him now I know how far in the gutter his imagination lives. Then again, I'm keen to join him there because I am already planning on escaping to read book number three.

I must have been sitting there for a good thirty minutes before he enters the room looking tired and dishevelled and my heart flutters at the sight of him. His hair is messy and begs for my touch to comb it into shape with my fingers. His eyes look tired and there is a sexy stubble on his face that calls to the woman in me. He is wearing a warm jumper with jeans that demonstrate a casual chic that looks good on the sort of men that grace the covers of magazines the world over. Yes, Leo Bradshaw is God's gift to women, and I can't wait to unwrap him.

He smiles as he grabs his coffee and a croissant and joins me and I sit up a little straighter and inadvertently lean forward to demonstrate my attractive qualities.

He throws me a curious look before groaning. "It's been a while since I threw an all-nighter."

He laughs at the confusion on my face and adds some

sugar to his tea, and winks. "For energy. I was up all night editing just to get the story finished. I'll suffer for it today though. I doubt I'll be good for much and may just head back to bed after breakfast."

Resisting telling him I'll join him and help with his energy levels, I resort to licking marmalade suggestively off my fingers while staring into his dark, compelling eyes. Leaning forward, I say somewhat huskily, "Yes, I could certainly do with a lie down myself."

He doesn't even blink and says with surprise, "Couldn't you sleep?"

Running my fingers through my hair, I lower my lashes and then look up through them and giggle like a stupid idiot. "No, I didn't get much sleep. I mean, all that tossing and turning, writhing and stretching, kept me up all night."

He looks at me curiously and takes a bite of his croissant before looking around. "I must be either early or late because there are still quite a few missing."

Feeling a little frustrated that he can't see the woman begging for amorous attention right in front of his eyes, I say snappily, "Well, they are on holiday."

He nods and then jumps up, saying sweetly, "Maybe we could both use a good meal inside us. What do you say, one sausage or two?"

Batting my lashes, I say suggestively, "Just one big, fat, juicy sausage for me. I'm sure that will satisfy my hunger."

He smiles and heads off, and I wonder if I'm doing this right. I may as well have asked for a bowl of cornflakes due to the reaction I just got.

I hear someone laughing and look up to see Brenda watching me. She grins and then heads over and takes Leo's vacant chair and leans forward. "Listen, honey, you're playing this all wrong."

"Playing what?"

She shakes her head and laughs softly. "It reminded me of when I was a dancer at the Moulin Rouge." She grins. "Well, I was quite inexperienced in the ways of a woman due to the fact I was fresh out of the convent. Anyway, I soon got the hang of managing the customer's expectations and learned to use my natural assets in a far cleverer way."

I just stare at Brenda as is becoming the habit, and she lowers her voice. "You're being a little over the top, if I may say. Now, that man looks wrecked and not in a good way. You could stand naked on the table dressed only in a fig leaf and he wouldn't blink an eye. He may be walking and talking, but his senses have deserted him. No, you need to rein it in and mother him a bit. Fuss over him because men love that. Once he feels cared for and comfortable, his libido will wake up and smell the coffee. Then the siren in you makes an appearance, but in a demure, shy, intoxicating way. He needs to feel as if he is the hunter and you are the prey. At the moment it's all on a plate for him and where's the fun in that? No dear, play hard to get for a little while longer and allow him to think the whole thing is his idea. It works every time and I wouldn't have got as far as I did in the bright lights of Paris if I didn't know how to manipulate a man to do my bidding."

I think I stare open-mouthed as she winks and joins Colin and I hear her say loudly, "Eat up, Colin, you're getting a little paunchy these days and we need to go for a jog around the island to shift the pounds."

Trying not to imagine the portly pair in lycra, I sink back in my seat and feel a complete failure. I can't even entice a man who has sex on the brain 24/7. This is a disaster. I wish Rita was here. She would know what I need to do.

CHAPTER 29

To my extreme frustration, after breakfast Leo heads back to bed – alone, leaving me to my own devices. Deciding the best use of my time would be to help Marigold clear away the breakfast dishes, I head off to look for her.

I find her sitting in the kitchen with a well-deserved mug of coffee and a bacon sandwich, and she smiles as I drag a chair up to the bench to join her.

"Morning, Scarlett, you're looking very nice today."

I smile weakly and help myself to coffee, wishing the word nice had been replaced with chic, elegant, sexy, in fact, anything but nice. Sighing, I decide I have a lot to learn and Marigold regards me thoughtfully.

"Tell me what's bothering you?"

I look up and say sadly, "It's hard trying to be something you're not but very much want to be."

She smiles sweetly and I groan. "You see, Marigold, when I came here, it was to escape from a situation I no longer wanted because I was too weak to deal with it. Now I'm here, I'm finding things out about myself that shock and excite me at the same time, but once again, I don't know what to do about it. How do people know what the right thing to do is? I mean, is there a manual somewhere on living your best life? Am I trying too hard and should I just back off and let nature take its course?"

She leans forward and says softly, "I expect you're talking about Leo."

I nod miserably as she sits back and smiles sympathetically. "In my experience, I would let nature take its course. Maybe you're trying to force a situation that would play out better naturally. I don't think you have anything to worry about on that score because it's obvious he likes you. That's plain for everyone to see. The thing is dear, he's an experienced man and you are younger than him and just finding yourself. My advice would be to just relax and enjoy the whole experience because I'm guessing you have absolutely nothing to worry about."

Smiling gratefully, I relax a little and then wonder if I should ask, but can't seem to help myself. "Um... Marigold, what's the story with Ryan?"

I feel myself blush as she raises her eyes and I say quickly, "I mean, he's a good-looking guy and well, I just wondered why he appears to be single."

Laughing, she rolls her eyes. "That one is enjoying himself way too much. He loves the ladies and his eyes are bigger than his libido. I've lost count of all the women who he's taken a fancy to and why not? He's still young and finding his way too."

"But what if he was to meet someone who he really likes? What then? I mean, what if she was wrong for him? How would you deal with that?"

Marigold smiles a little sadly. "You don't need to worry about Ryan, Scarlett. He knows how things are and if he gets a little happiness thrown in along the way, then I'm grateful for it."

She stands and starts clearing the remnants of her breakfast and says lightly, "Anyway, I have food to prepare. I have a wedding feast to organise and nothing makes me happier than that."

Remembering that it's Christmas Eve tomorrow, I think about what needs to be done and say keenly, "Would you like a hand?"

"It's fine. To be honest, most of it is done already and safely in the fridge and freezer. Maybe Phoebe would like a hand with the decorations, or Fiona with her dress and stuff. Thanks for the offer though."

Leaving Marigold behind, it strikes me there's a sadness to her that no amount of smiles can disguise. In fact, the more I come to think of it, Ryan has that same look in his eyes. They are two of the nicest people in the world, but they also seem the loneliest. I wonder what the future holds for them because, like me, it's an uncertain one. In fact, when I think about it, we are all here on shaky ground. Nobody here lives the perfect life, and it appears many have just brought their excess baggage with them.

I find Phoebe in the lounge writing in a large notebook, and she looks up when she sees me coming.

"Hi, Scarlett, it's a lovely day today."

Looking at the bright blue sky outside, I have to agree with her. "It certainly is. Do you think we'll have snow for Christmas? It's certainly cold enough."

"I hope so. Jamie would love that."

She lowers her eyes and looks a little sad and I can tell something's the matter, so I sit beside her and say gently, "Can I help you with anything?"

"Not really. You see, just before we came to Holly Island,

Kevin found out that his job was unlikely to still be there when we returned."

Her eyes fill with tears and she looks out of the window with a sad expression. "It's not just the job, either. Money's been tight for a while, what with one thing and another, and I tried to help by getting a job myself, but there's nothing suitable that allows me to work around Jamie's school. Rebecca's Uni fees are quite high and Kevin insists on paying for them and Christmas was something we couldn't really afford."

She sighs heavily. "We just wanted a nice family Christmas somewhere special, and this one was too good an offer to pass by. We paid so little for it compared to what we would spend at home and now it appears we shouldn't even have done that. We have credit card bills that are out of control and the payments are on shaky ground. Our mortgage repayments are rising because Kevin keeps on taking out more money and we have had to try to cut back. That's why it's doubtful we could take Jasper back with us. Pets can be expensive and it is money we haven't got right now. To cap it all, we haven't managed to spend much on the Christmas presents this year and so any we have bought aren't the usual high-tech and designer brands the kids want these days. I'm just worried that Jamie will have a miserable Christmas day when he sees that Santa's on a budget this year."

I feel bad for her and try to rack my brains to think of a way out of it, but anything I think of sounds ridiculous and shallow. Instead, I say sympathetically, "It must be difficult for you. When will you know for sure about Kevin's job?"

"When we return, I suppose after the New Year. There was talk of them being bought out by a foreign investor, so fingers crossed that happens."

Looking at the notebook she's writing in, I see a list of

some description and she sees me looking and smiles. "The list of things to do for Fiona's big day tomorrow. I thought I'd try to make it magical and would quite enjoy doing it. If anything, it will take my mind off my own situation for a couple of days, anyway."

"I can help you if you like. I would quite enjoy decorating for a wedding, especially a winter one."

She nods gratefully and I watch as she appears to dust off her sadness and says briskly, "Let's start by visiting that attic where they store the decorations. Who knows what we may find?"

I follow her outside and feel bad. Life can be so cruel at times, and I wonder if things will improve for them. I certainly hope so because they are nice people and deserve a little happiness. Then I worry about Jasper because if Jamie has to leave him behind, it will break everyone's heart.

Once again, I feel the weight of everyone's problems on my own weak shoulders. Maybe a good session with Leo is what's needed to drive the demons out. Then again, I wouldn't know what that involves and would probably get that wrong as well. Not for the first time I wish Rita was here. She would know what to do. She's a pro at this.

CHAPTER 30

*T*he attic is just as I remember it, dark, dusty and full of spiders and dirty cobwebs.

The air smells stale and the floorboards creak under the weight of all the piles of clutter and broken items that litter the floor.

Phoebe looks around in excitement and squeals, "Oh my god, this place is amazing."

"If you say so." I brush a cobweb from my face and shiver as I think of all the scurrying creatures that live here, waiting to attack us at any moment.

Phoebe, though, is enchanted and moves around the attic like a woman possessed. Soon she starts pulling out various items and thrusting them towards me. "Here, take these to the top of the stairs. We'll form a pile and get the others to help us carry them down later."

I do as I'm told as piles of fabric, various objects and what appear to be even more decorations are thrust into my aching arms and we soon have quite the collection. Phoebe's in her element and her delighted chatter lights up the usually dead space as she breathes new life into objects that are well past their best.

I think we must spend a good hour in the attic and I am relieved when she says with satisfaction, "There, I think that should start us off."

Grabbing a huge box, she nods towards a heap of fabric and says eagerly, "If you bring that pile, we can start sorting it out in the library. It will be such fun seeing ways to transform it into a fantastic wedding venue."

"Is that where they're having it, then?"

"Yes, we spoke about it yesterday. It's got a great atmosphere and an amazing view out of the huge, leaded window, that frames the sea outside. There's space to set up some chairs and the large desk at the end is perfect for the couple to sit at as they pose for pictures and say their vows."

"Any news on the priest yet?"

Phoebe's face falls and she whispers, "I've got a bad feeling about that. Kevin says that Martin is convinced the one they booked won't let them down, but it still worries me."

"I'm sure it will be fine. After all, if you can't trust a priest, who can you trust?"

Phoebe laughs and I follow her downstairs, feeling quite excited about the day ahead.

By the time we have mustered every available strong pair of arms, we have quite the collection in the library. Phoebe, Rebecca, Fiona and I look with excitement at the odd group of objects and Fiona shakes her head. "It all looks a little mismatched. Are you sure it won't look tacky?"

Phoebe rolls her eyes and makes a clucking sound, causing Rebecca to hide a grin. "Honestly, Fiona, you can rest assure that we will produce your dream wedding."

Suddenly, Brenda heads into the room and says loudly,

"Goodness, you have all been busy. Now, we don't have long and if this is to go like clockwork, we need to get a move on."

She looks around and then down at her clipboard. "Right then, Rebecca, you are in charge of hair and make-up. Maybe you would like to take Fiona off for a practice."

Fiona looks a little relieved and follows a smiling Rebecca out of the room. Then Brenda says happily, "There, that got rid of the bride. It's always best to distract them from the general details because they only cast an anxious shadow over the whole event. It was much the same when I used to help out at the celebrity weddings organised by OK magazine. Goodness, the tantrums those Divas threw caused me no end of problems. It was touch and go on a few, but luckily, I managed to save the big day on many an occasion. Now, where was I?"

Phoebe catches my eye and grins, and I stifle mine. I could listen to her all day long, even if she is stretching the truth most of the time.

Brenda says loudly, "Anyway, if I may leave you both to your work, I need to liaise with Marigold and see how the wedding cake's coming on. Hopefully, she's done as I asked and I won't have to stay up half the night recreating the one that won me my heat on MasterChef."

She heads out of the room and Phoebe says incredulously, "Do you believe anything that woman says because I know I don't."

Laughing, I start unpacking one of the boxes. "If she is telling the truth, she should be the one writing the books instead of Leo. Even if I'd done a fraction of the things she has, I would die a happy woman."

As we work, I find a newfound respect for Phoebe. The piles of fabric reveal beautiful ivory silk curtains that she soon has re-formed into beautiful covers for the chairs that she's set up in rows facing the window. Another piece of red satin fabric is soon split into lengths to tie around the backs of the chairs and into bows. Somehow, she has found a box of fairy lights and we string them around the room, leaving no wall space unfilled, as we entwine them with ivy found in the garden and little sprigs of holly and mistletoe tied on by tiny white strips of silk.

We carefully place church candles in glass jars around the room and tie bunches of mistletoe to every mirror and picture. Phoebe is so excited to have found some absolutely huge candelabras and I watch her decorate them with fresh foliage and insert candles in the holders.

The room looks enchanting when we finish and I say with admiration, "You are so good at this, Phoebe. Have you done this sort of thing before professionally?"

She rolls her eyes and looks a little embarrassed. "No, but I've always been interested in decorating for events."

"Then you should look into making it a career. I think you're very good and could have quite a successful business if you put your mind to it."

We look at the left-over boxes from the attic and Phoebe pulls out a pile of what appears to be forgotten clothes. As she holds them up, we gasp in amazement at the sight of the most beautiful ball gowns and suits that look as if they belong in the last century. We are like two little girls in a candy store because these dresses, despite smelling old and musty, are truly beautiful.

I say with excitement, "We should clean these up and see if they fit. Wouldn't it be lovely to wear them tomorrow?"

Phoebe nods and pulls a beautiful satin, pale blue gown from the box, with an impressive underskirt. The delicate embroidery on the bodice looks to be the work of an accomplished seamstress, and she holds the dress against her and gasps, "I love this one so much. Do you think there's enough for everyone?"

Quickly, we sort through the remaining boxes and must pull out at least six dresses and six suits. I rummage through the rest but can't find any more and feel a little disappointed. "There's not enough."

"Then we should go back and check the attic. You never know, we may find some."

Quickly, we head back to the stairs and almost run to the attic. This time, I don't see the cobwebs and evil creatures waiting to pounce on me. This time I don't even wait for my eyes to adjust to the dim light because I am too busy pulling down boxes and opening them like a woman possessed. It must be fifteen minutes later that I shout triumphantly, "I think I have some."

Phoebe helps me lift the heavy trunk off the shelf and we don't even wait and open it eagerly. Inside are several more dresses and suits and one, in particular, catches my eye. As I hold it up, Phoebe's eyes shine in the dim light and she gasps, "It's perfect."

As I stroke the soft silk, I have to agree. Now we just need to clean them up and distribute them among the other guests.

We enlist the help of Marigold, who laughs when she sees what we found. "Goodness, I completely forgot about these. They will need a good clean and maybe some alterations. Leave it with me and I'll have them ready for the morning."

"We'll help you, won't we, Phoebe?"

Phoebe nods, and Marigold shakes her head. "It's fine. If I need you, I'll come and find you. Now, if I'm not mistaken, Scarlett, I think Leo is looking for you and Jamie has just got back from his walk with Kevin and Jasper. Maybe you could see if they need a hot drink and some water for Jasper."

Feeling a little bad, we leave Marigold with what appears to be a mammoth task, and as we walk to meet the others,

Phoebe says happily, "Thank you, Scarlett. I've had the best day and you've given me a good idea."

"What, the wedding planning?"

She nods. "Among other things. Maybe we can look at setting something up when we get home. Who knows, it may just be what I've been looking for?"

I spy Leo walking towards me and resist the urge to run to him because, after his rest, Leo looks amazing. He smiles as he sees me coming, and Phoebe laughs softly. "You make a lovely couple. Maybe you will be my second wedding."

I feel my face flush as she giggles and heads off to find her family. Goodness, marriage to a man like that, if only dreams do come true.

CHAPTER 31

*L*eo and I head outside for a long walk and it feels good to walk with his hand in mine. It's a lovely day and if there was ever a perfect winter's day, this is it. The sky is bright blue with not a cloud to spoil it and the sea is calm and sparkles with the sun's reflection.

The air is crisp and cold and yet the sun's rays warm my face as we walk side by side down towards the water's edge.

Leo is good company and we discover lots of shared interests, reading in particular, and then he says, "What did you think of the book; which one did you choose in the end?"

I should have anticipated his question, but I completely forgot about the effect his book had on me for a while and now it all comes rushing back and I remember the feelings it stirred up.

Grateful that he can't see my face, I say lightly, "It was, um... interesting."

"Just interesting."

I detect a slight edge to his voice and realise how important this is to him. Stopping, I turn to face him and say earnestly, "I loved it, Leo. I'm surprised that I did, but I couldn't put it down. In fact, I woke a few hours later and read another. You are very talented."

His eyes widen and he looks in shock for a moment and then a broad smile breaks out across his face and he smiles happily. "You liked it – them. That means a lot."

He looks so happy I catch my breath because Leo is much more than an extremely attractive man. He is kind, amusing and good company and I can't believe I've met him and he appears to like me too. I watch as his smile turns to a look of intensity that steals my breath and freezes it in time. This moment appears in slow motion and the only thing that moves is the steady thump of my heart as he says softly, "I meant what I said yesterday. I want to leave Holly Island with you beside me. I never expected to find someone while running from another and yet, here you are."

I nod and say with a slight quiver in my voice. "Yes, here we are. Both running and as luck would have it to the same place."

He takes my hand and I just wish I didn't have a pair of ski gloves keeping my skin from touching his, as he says solemnly, "You will leave with me, won't you? I want to introduce you to my friends, my family, and my world. I want to meet your family and friends and somehow make a life together. I know it is early days but I feel so strongly about this. It's as if Holly Island has cast a spell over me and bewitched me into falling in love with you."

I stare at him in shock – love!

The tears glisten in my eyes as he pulls me close and kisses me gently. My mind swirls with a million thoughts and all of them good. Life doesn't seem real on Holly Island. Everything is better, bigger and more pronounced. Could this just be as a result of that? However, as I kiss Leo, standing by the ocean, I feel him claim my heart. We could be anywhere and I would feel this connection. I just know I would.

We walk back towards the hotel with a new understanding formed between us. We walk back as a couple, an item, and a man and woman in love. I leave every doubt I had firmly behind me and face the future without fear. My mind is made up. I love Leo too and now I have no doubts about taking it to the next stage because it's the most natural thing to do.

We return to the hotel and it feels as if we've come home to the strangest family anyone could ever imagine having. The first people we see are Harold and Alice and they are dancing the waltz in the hallway. Harold laughs as he sees us and winks. "Just practising for tomorrow. It should be a day to remember."

Alice grins at me and I hope she gets what she wants because they make a good couple. I wonder how she'll approach it. Maybe Harold is happy playing the field and she'll be disappointed; I certainly hope not.

We head into the bar to make ourselves a cocktail or two and see Fiona pouring herself a large brandy. She looks a little preoccupied and, as we approach, looks up and smiles shakily. "Oh, hi guys. Can I interest either of you in a brandy?"

Leo shakes his head and joins her behind the bar. "No, we both fancy a cocktail before dinner. Would you like me to rustle one up for you? I'm a dab hand at a porn star martini."

I laugh out loud at her expression and roll my eyes. "Of course you are, Leo." I nod to a couple of wing-backed chairs by the open fire and Fiona follows me.

While Leo plays at being a cocktail waiter, I sense that all is not well with Fiona and say in a low voice, "Are you nervous?"

She looks surprised and I add, "About tomorrow, I mean."

Taking a sip of her brandy, she shrugs. "It's not as if I haven't done it before."

"That's not what I asked."

I'm slightly worried to see tears form in her eyes and she blinks them away. "I don't know, maybe I just think we're rushing into this 'happy ever after, I forgive you,' vow renewal. Martin and I have always done this. We don't speak about our feelings and just gloss over the cracks. The thing is, though, those cracks are still there and make an unwelcome appearance from time to time. Is that normal? I kind of think it is because if I speak to any of my friends, all they do is moan about their husbands and speak of them badly. Am I expecting too much and chasing something that dims over time?"

Feeling a little alarmed at her words, I shrug. "I don't know. I'm not the best person to ask. I've only ever had one relationship before coming here, but as I think about it, I can sort of relate to what you're saying. We were one another's first loves. We met when I was still at school and sort of did everything we thought was expected of a boyfriend and girlfriend. It took me a long time to even find him, so I pushed aside the feeling that something wasn't right and just accepted that was how things were. However, it was always there at the back of my mind. It just didn't feel right, which is why I panicked when I thought he was going to propose."

Fiona looks interested as I look across at Leo working away making the drinks and I smile happily. "Then I came here and met Leo. It was instant – the connection we shared. It made me realise that the relationship I had with Gregory was wrong on every level. I had feelings I never knew existed and I know that sounds cliché, but it's true. Gregory and I were just going through the motions, and it scares me just how close I came to doing the wrong thing. I do kind of understand where you're coming from, but only you can really decide what you want. Maybe you should take a moment to imagine how you would feel if you weren't with Martin. Picture him meeting someone else. How would that make you feel? If you didn't have him in your life, would it bother you? Like I said, I'm no expert on this, but this is an important decision you're making and shouldn't be entered into lightly."

Leo heads over, looking extremely pleased with himself, and hands us both a cocktail. "Porn star anyone?"

Fiona laughs. "Now there's an offer."

Laughing, we clink glasses and as we take a sip, I catch her eye and she nods. I can tell I've given her something to think about at least and just hope I haven't ruined what promises to be an amazing day tomorrow. More than anything, I want to dress up in one of those fabulous costumes and see Leo standing beside me in the suit we found. I want to experience the magic of the ceremony performed in the romantic setting that Phoebe has provided and I want to dance in Leo's arms to the sound of romantic music and make a happy memory when everything is new and exciting. It will be such an inconvenience if the day is cancelled but then again, nowhere near as inconvenient as a life spent regretting a wrong decision.

CHAPTER 32

*T*onight, it's my turn to help Marigold with dinner and as we work away in the professional kitchen; it strikes me that this dream is coming to an end sooner than I would like it to. It's Christmas Eve tomorrow and we only have four days left before the elusive departure boat arrives to take us all back to civilisation.

Marigold must sense I'm feeling a little low and I catch her looking at me with concern a few times before saying, "Have you enjoyed your stay here, Scarlett?"

"I have, thank you." I think about what four days' time means to Marigold and feel bad. "What about you? What will you do?"

She smiles and I notice not one trace of worry in her eyes, just an acceptance of a situation out of her control. "You don't have to worry about us. Our future was determined a long time ago. Holly Island is a magical place and will always be a part of us. Whatever happens in the future, we will always belong here."

It strikes me that she doesn't look worried at all and I

wonder if she has found another job. "What will you do when we leave?"

"Tidy up I suppose." She rolls her eyes and laughs softly. "It will certainly feel strange when you all go home."

I feel worried for her and say gently, "Have you thought about, um... well, the future?"

"I stopped thinking of the future years ago, Scarlett. It's just important to learn to enjoy every minute of your life. Be happy now. Time is precious, I've learned that the hard way. Some aspects of our life we can control, others not. It's just important to embrace change and do what makes you happy. People come and go. It's inevitable. However, you remain the only constant in your life and it's imperative you do what's right for you. Whatever happens next for me, I'll be ready and will adapt to change – I have no other choice."

I take a moment for her words to sink in and know she's right. It doesn't take away the worry though, but it's a plan at least.

I still have some doubts, though. "But how do you know that you're making the right decision?"

Her eyes soften. "You will know. I'm guessing you are referring to Leo. Well, in my humble opinion, true love doesn't happen right away; it develops over time after you have experienced many ups and downs, when you've suffered together, cried together and laughed together. Only then can you judge whether that love has stood the test of time. Take Fiona and Martin, for example. They are renewing their vows because they want to put the past behind them and move on together. It hasn't been easy for them and they may not have made it, but they have decided to put their problems in the past and walk together hand in hand into the future. You never know what life will throw at you, but you must have a starting point at least."

I'm not sure how the conversation changed from

Marigold's current situation to mine, but she looks at the time and laughs. "Goodness, I can't stand around here chatting all day. I have 101 things to do before the ceremony tomorrow. Let's get this dinner served and maybe I can grab some time this evening to make a start."

She turns away and I think about what she said. Are there any guarantees in life? I already know the answer to that. However, at least, as she said, I have a starting point and what a fine one it is.

The evening is a quiet one for a change. We all ate far too much and drank so much alcohol, everyone is feeling sleepy and just lounging about by the roaring fire. Rebecca is playing a board game with Jamie while they toast marshmallows on the fire. Harold is snoring on the settee, his head on Alice's shoulder. She appears to be knitting some kind of garment, although God only knows what, and Kevin's reading a book. Phoebe has left to put the final touches to the room and Fiona and Martin appear to be missing in action.

Brenda and Colin are playing cards and I'm curled up next to Leo and relish the fact that he is rubbing my shoulder as we listen to carols on the radio. Maybe it's because there's no television or that we are just bored rigid, but Alice suddenly starts to sing along with the carol Silent Night, causing the rest of us to join in. There is something so magical about sitting together doing things the old-fashioned way, but as the candles burn all around us and the fire dances in time to our voices, I can't ever remember a Christmas as perfect as this one.

WHEN I WAKE the next morning, it's wrapped in Leo's arms. Although we spent the night together, it was all perfectly innocent and above board. We were content just to talk long into the night and share our hopes for the future. We stole the odd kiss here and there, and it just made me fall in love with him a little more.

We are not keen to rush something that is inevitable in the long run. Taking things slowly just heightens the anticipation and makes me feel even more comfortable around him.

I can tell it's early because the room is still bathed in a dusty grey light. A quick glance at the clock by the bed tells me it's 6 am and I smile to myself. I have always loved Christmas Eve because usually everything is wrapped and waiting patiently under the tree for the onslaught of Christmas Day. The cards are written and sent and the tree and decorations sit proudly waiting for their big day. The cupboards groan under the weight of all the food and every available cupboard and surface is taken up with Christmas.

Christmas puddings were made weeks, if not months ago, and the Christmas cake sits proudly underneath a glass dome. Christmas songs play on the radio and there is a heightened excitement in the air as the countdown begins.

However, this Christmas Eve is special for a different reason entirely. Today will be one of a kind and very special because I will attend my first vow renewal ceremony and by the looks of things, it will be beautiful.

I feel excited and shake Leo, whispering, "Wake up, Leo, it's Christmas Eve."

He groans and pulls the covers a little tighter over his head. "Just a few moments longer."

Giggling, I pull the duvet away and say in a loud voice, "Come on, let's go and watch the sunrise."

Shaking his head, Leo sits up and runs his fingers through his hair and looks at the clock. "Scarlett, it's still the middle of the night and I doubt the sun will even show its face, can't you hear the rain outside?"

"What?"

I listen keenly and then, with dismay, spring from the bed and pull back the curtains, revealing a window plastered with rain and the sound of the wind howling through the trees.

Laughing softly, Leo wraps himself in the duvet and says happily, "As I said, it's the middle of the night. I'm going back to sleep."

Gloomily, I press my face against the window and watch the landscape cope with a battering. Great, this isn't how it was supposed to be. Poor Fiona, what a horrible day.

Then I think of the splendid room that Phoebe created and cheer up a bit. It doesn't matter that the weather is being unkind, we don't need to go outside, anyway.

Feeling a little brighter, I pull on my jeans and a warm jumper and find my cosy, fluffy slippers and then whisper, "I'm going to grab a cup of tea, do you want one?"

The only response I get is a groan and, shrugging, I head outside, intent on heading straight to the kitchen.

I try to be as quiet as a church mouse because as I pass the various occupied rooms, I hear gentle snoring providing the dawn chorus. I laugh to myself as I head downstairs, but as I pass the room at the end of the hallway, something catches my eye and I stop and stare.

I know this is one of the empty rooms and so the curiosity gets the better of me. What's in there?

As I push open the door, I gasp in amazement and just stare as the sight before me takes my breath away. Then I can think of nothing else but my need to go inside and the tea can wait.

CHAPTER 33

*A*ll around me hang the most beautiful dresses I have ever seen. It's like walking into Cinderella's Fairy Godmother's imagination. The crumpled, dusty costumes we found in the attic yesterday have been totally transformed into a scene from Cinderella's ball. I don't know which one to look at first and grasp the nearest one with a hunger I have never felt for fashion before.

The silk runs through my fingers with the gentlest of touches. The deep red silk is offset by an embroidered corset decorated with sparkling jewels. Braiding enhances the curves and then nips in at waist where the skirt flares out, under which sits metres of netting. I can't wait and quickly remove my clothing, aching to feel the caress of the most beautiful dress I have ever seen in my life. As I step into a garment I have only ever seen in movies, I tremble as I feel transformed. I feel like a princess – no, a Queen. It fits me perfectly and as I dance around the room; I feel as if Christmas has come early.

I feel amazing and quickly race to the mirror in the corner of the room to check that it looks as good as it feels.

The image staring back at me is of a girl I don't recognise. This girl – no woman - has excitement in her eyes. Her face is devoid of make-up but glows with a beauty no make-up can enhance. I feel beautiful and it shows, to me, anyway.

I laugh like a child on Christmas morning. How did she do this? How did Marigold work such magic? She must have worked through the night because surely this would take a team of seamstresses' months to achieve? However, Marigold has worked a miracle and this perfect day has started in the best possible way.

As I look around the room, I see the one dress that stood out from the others. What I very much hope will be Fiona's wedding gown. A beautiful ivory silk dress with intricate lace detail. It dazzles as the gems that have been sewn into the fabric sparkle in the light. It almost looks alive as it shimmers brighter than all the others and I pray that it fits because Fiona will feel like a princess in that dress and she deserves it. This is her day, and she should have the very best of everything.

I almost can't wait for the others to wake up because I want to share this with them all. Even the men's suits look splendid as they stand to attention on their hangers while guarding the dresses. They are made from the richest wool fabric and are adorned with brass and embroidery. Prince Charming could have designed these himself because they wouldn't look out of place at the palace ball. I almost can't cope with it all and must spend a good hour just trying all the dresses on and losing myself in the past.

Reluctantly, I head downstairs to make the tea and think about the day ahead. I believe the ceremony is due to go ahead at 2 pm and there is a lot to do beforehand.

As I make the tea, Marigold appears and I notice how weary she looks. "My goodness, you must have been up all night."

She nods. "I was, but it was successful. Everything is ready and hopefully, the day will go without a hitch."

I shake my head and say in wonder, "You are so clever, Marigold. I saw the dresses and the suits and they took my breath away. How did you do it?"

She smiles a secret smile and says softly, "When you enjoy doing something, it's not a chore. Somehow, you get the energy to do the impossible. I loved every minute of restoring those dresses and will look forward to seeing them brought to life again."

She turns to start preparing breakfast and I say firmly, "Back to bed - immediately."

Looking surprised, she shakes her head. "I can't. What about breakfast?"

"I'll organise breakfast. It's the least I can do. Now, I don't want to see you until midday. I'll bring you a cup of tea to your room and then you can get ready for the wedding, as a guest."

She looks shocked but can obviously see that I'm not taking no for an answer, so she smiles gratefully. "Ok, it would be good to get some sleep – thank you."

She heads off to bed and I start my own preparations instead. Yes, sometimes it's important to do the right thing and as the first one up, I think it's only right that I help out.

As the guests start to drift down one by one, I can't contain my excitement. The women, of course, are more excited than the men and over breakfast, we chatter across the room discussing the plans for the day that involves nothing but the wedding. I think the excitement is contagious because even Jasper must sense it because he has taken to racing around the room at 100 mph and dodging in between the tables and generally creating mayhem.

Leo joins me and I fill him in and he looks interested.

"Am I expected to wear one of those suits? I'm not sure if I like the sound of it if I'm honest."

"You say that now, but wait until you see them. Honestly, Leo, this memory will stay with you forever. I don't think I've ever seen clothes like them and it's doubtful you could hire them on the mainland. They are that special."

He doesn't look convinced but I can't dwell on that right now because Martin and Fiona finally emerge amid many cheers and well wishes. I'm pleased to see that Fiona seems a little brighter, and I jump up and head over to their table. "Morning guys, the big day has finally arrived. Now, it's my turn to prepare breakfast, so what can I get you?"

I take their orders for a full cooked breakfast and notice that Martin is looking particularly pleased with himself. I'm not sure why, but ever since our chat in the woods, I've been a little put off him. Maybe it was because he told a lie against his own brother to steal his girlfriend - yes, it must be that because that was a low blow. It's also his attitude to Fiona. He seems to love the fact that she feels guilty about cheating on him much more than he feels betrayed. I still feel uncomfortable about the whole thing because, to an outsider, there is something very wrong with their relationship.

I head off to prepare their breakfast and push my own views aside. It doesn't matter what I think, anyway, only what they think counts, so I busy myself with doing something to help rather than hinder and just feel grateful that I'm a part of this at all.

As soon as breakfast is over, Brenda takes charge and stands with her clipboard, issuing her orders like the wedding planner she has appointed herself to be.

Along with the rest of the guests, I am instructed to form an orderly queue outside the 'dressing room' as Brenda puts it, where my outfit will be given to me. Fiona is to be given the first choice, although there is really only one choice as far as I'm concerned. She would be mad not to choose the ivory silk gown because it stands head and shoulders above the rest of them.

The men are instructed to make sure there are enough logs for the fires and to keep Martin out of mischief, as Brenda put it. I'm pretty sure they all disappear off to the bar, which doesn't surprise me because it's where they all appear to live most days, anyway.

I find myself standing behind Rebecca and she looks at me with excitement.

"I can't wait to see the dresses; are they really that good?"

I nod enthusiastically. "Better. Honestly, Rebecca, you won't ever get to wear the likes of it again, I'm sure of that. They are out of this world and I'm not exaggerating."

She looks excited. "I can't wait. You know, Scarlett, I was dreading coming here. I think you know that. When my father told me we were coming, I tried everything I knew to get out of it. He wouldn't take no for an answer, and I'm kind of glad he didn't. This trip has opened my eyes – a lot. I came here as a sullen teenager and am leaving a woman."

My heart sinks and I can't stop the images that come back with a vengeance. Surely not, I couldn't bear it and I say tentatively, "That's good, what made you change?"

She laughs and taps the side of her nose. "All in good time. It must stay a secret for a little longer and like all Christmas surprises, can only be opened on Christmas Day."

I watch her enter the room to choose her dress and think about what I know. She certainly has a secret, that's not in any doubt, but what could it be? Does it concern Harold or Ryan, both or neither? I hope it's a nice surprise though, because I've grown to care for the slightly dysfunctional family that have many hurdles to jump.

It surprises me that when each one of the guests enters the room, not one of them comes out. It annoys me a little because I want to see what dress they chose and just hope it isn't the scarlet one I want. Ever since I saw it, I can't get it out of my mind. It's perfect for me and I know it shouldn't matter because they were all lovely, but I have really set my heart on that dress.

I'm not sure why I was asked to wait until last, and I feel a little miffed about it. I know that Fiona should get the first choice, of course, she should, but I am technically the maid of honour, so surely, I should be next.

Shifting anxiously from side to side, I count down in my head the seconds that turn into minutes until I hear, "Scarlett, you can come in now."

CHAPTER 34

As I enter the room, I'm surprised to see that's its empty except for Brenda standing with her ever-present clipboard. She notices my surprise and says matter-of-factly, "Connecting door. It was easier to let everyone leave that way and as the connecting room opens around the corner, it kept the hall traffic to a minimum."

With excitement, I look around the room, but aside from the rows of men's suits hanging proudly waiting to be claimed, the only dress I see makes my heart sink. Purple!

I try to hide it, but Brenda can obviously sense that I'm disappointed and says sympathetically, "I'm sorry, it's always tough being the last one. Never mind dear, if it's any consolation, I think you'll look amazing in this dress. The colour is rich and decadent and will suit your skin tone. The embroidery on it is the best I've ever seen, and the skirt is much fuller than the others."

She looks around and then, as if from thin air, produces a lovely pair of satin heels that I have never seen before. "Here, Marigold found some shoes in another trunk and it looks as if these match your dress."

I look at the outfit with a critical eye and then it occurs to me, "What if they don't fit?"

Brenda winks. "Like all fairy tales, my dear, I'm sure they will. Now, if you don't mind, I have a million things to accomplish before the witching hour. Could you call the men to form an orderly line and I'll deal with them on a one by one basis?"

She winks, and I stifle a grin. Sighing, I gather up my treasure and reason with myself. Despite not being the outfit of my choice, it is still singularly the best dress I have ever worn in my life, and I feel excited to slip it over my head and experience what it must have been like for a woman of the past.

As I head through the connecting door, I laugh to myself. Holly Island is full of surprises and I never thought for one moment I would be doing this. I'm glad I am though and can't believe how I nearly passed up the chance to experience this whole fairy tale.

I still feel a little guilty about the fact I let everyone down, but sometimes it's important just to throw caution to the wind and do what makes you happy.

I see Colin heading towards me and smile. "Just the man. Colin, would you be so kind as to ask the men to form an orderly queue outside room 34? Brenda is waiting to deal with them, as she put it."

Colin laughs and winks. "It wouldn't be the first time I've had that instruction."

I stare after him in shock, not knowing if he was joking or not, but then again, anything that couple do shouldn't surprise me. They are definitely two of a kind.

For the next hour, I totally indulge my own comforts. Returning to my room, I take a deep soak in a perfumed bath and then shower off my hair. Wrapped in a cosy dressing gown, I try to make up my face in a way that would make any professional approve of it. Then I style my hair into a fancy up-do, with curls that hang down in little wisps, creating a romantic style that wouldn't look out of place in any period drama.

Then the moment I have been waiting for arrives and I start the process of transforming myself into a princess. As I slip the layers of silk fabric over my head, I feel the scratch of the underskirt as it travels down my body. As I shake a little, the folds fall into place and the lining acts as a silken barrier against the layers of netting. Lastly, I climb onto heels that miraculously fit and caress my feet, making me feel as if I'm walking on air.

Stepping back, I take a moment to stare at myself in wonder. Who is this girl staring back at me? She can't be me because she's beautiful. She glows with a radiance that I've never seen before and appears to stand a little taller, and her smile is a little brighter. Gone are the slightly rough edges and in their place is polished perfection. If Fairy Godmothers were real, mine would be standing beside me now. It doesn't matter that the dress wasn't my first choice because it is utter perfection.

A sharp knock interrupts my daydreaming and I call out, "Come in."

As the door opens, a sight fills the doorway that takes my breath away. Prince Charming is real and standing before me, looking at me with so much passion it makes me hold my breath. Leo's eyes glitter as he rakes me from head to toe and says roughly, "You are beautiful, Scarlett."

I blink away the tears because as moments go, this one is once in a lifetime. Leo is looking like the hero he is, resplendent in a royal blue velvet suit, edged with gold braiding, with crisp, white shirt and slim-fitting trousers, with a satin stripe down the side. If he was carrying a sword, it wouldn't look out of place and the expression in his eyes causes my heart to skip a beat.

He crosses the room in two long strides and, without a word, takes me in his arms and kisses me so intensely it makes me worry that my heart will burst. The air is supercharged with enough sexual chemistry to power Holly Island for an entire year. Then his hands encircle my waist and he pulls me as close as my dress will allow him and it strikes me that if any time was right to take this relationship to another level, it's this one.

However, despite the fact I want him to re-enact my bodice ripping fantasises, they will have to wait for another time because he pulls back and I am fascinated to see that his eyes have darkened until they are almost black and glitter dangerously. He stares at me for a moment and then growls in a deep, lust-filled voice, "I can't wait any longer, Scarlett, I want you to know how much you mean to me and I want to show you how good love can be."

I nod shyly and whisper, "I want that too, Leo. I don't want to wait for the right time because I think we've reached that point."

I see the emotion in his eyes as he pulls me close once again and kisses me so sweetly, I feel the emotion almost overwhelm me. I have never felt like this. I've read about it but never experienced the magic myself. I have never wanted anyone as I do him and so what if the timing sucks? You can't plan everything in life and life will just have to stop while we deal with the importance of finding our happy ever after.

Leo and I shut the world out.

We make time stand still and explore our new beginning.

Our clothes fall to the ground on top of our morals as we take a giant leap into the unknown.

Christmas Eve is a special time because it heralds the

beginning of something amazing, life-changing, and wonder-ful. It is the perfect time to look to the future with hope and an understanding that life will never be the same again because, from this day on, something has been born. It's the power of finding the person you were always meant to find and making that commitment to spend the rest of your life together.

The timing isn't perfect, but we can't help that.

The fact we should be somewhere else by now doesn't hold us back.

The ruined hair and make-up are a small price to pay.

The fact it's the middle of the day has no consequence.

Scarlett and Leo can't wait any longer because from the moment they met what happens next is inevitable.

CHAPTER 35

I feel so anxious. "Oh my goodness, we are so late."

"Stand still, I can't zip you up if you wriggle like this."

"Hurry up, Leo, I need to quickly do my hair again."

I feel his strong hands on my shoulders and melt under his touch as he spins me around and looks deep into my eyes. "No regrets?"

I shake my head and feel my eyes sparkle with the magic of experiencing true love for the very first time. "No regrets – you?"

His lips claim my own words and I melt against him. Pulling back, he whispers softly, "No regrets. I've wanted to do that since the first night we met. I was happy to wait until you were ready, but when I saw you in that dress looking so beautiful, I lost every ounce of control I had. I just hope you don't regret it because I couldn't live with myself if I thought you did."

I pull him tightly against me and almost want to cry. I can't deal with how deep my feelings for him have grown in such a short space of time. It's as if they established deep roots quickly and are now out of control.

Just for a moment, we stand clutching each other and then we hear someone yelling, "Scarlett, Leo, we're waiting for you."

Recognising Brenda's voice, we pull back and grin. Reaching up, Leo smoothes my hair away from my face and straightens my dress. Then he plants a soft kiss on my lips and, pulling back, offers me his arm. "Shall we?"

My heart beats faster as I take his arm and we walk out of my room together.

Brenda is waiting, and I see a mischievous twinkle in her eyes as she stares at us knowingly. Grinning, she says in a softer voice, "You both look gorgeous."

I stare at her in surprise because Brenda has transformed. She is wearing a golden dress that shimmers in the light. It's edged with ivory lace, and the bodice is intricately embroidered with pearls and silver gems. Her hair is styled into a chignon and is woven with little silver stars that glitter in the light and she looks about ten years younger, courtesy of the make-up she's wearing and the excitement on her face.

I can't help myself and gasp, "You look beautiful, Brenda."

I watch in fascination as a pink tinge travels to her cheeks and she waves her hands dismissively. "You're just being kind. Anyway, we should go. Martin is in position and we need to be waiting by the door with Rebecca and Jamie to follow Fiona up the aisle. Leo, you need to wait beside Martin."

As we walk, something occurs to me and I say quickly, "Did the Priest arrive?"

Brenda shakes her head. "Sadly not, my dear. You may not have noticed…" she winks and I blush a little, "That a severe storm has been raging for a good hour now. Unfortunately, no boat would be safe on those turbulent seas, so we've had to improvise."

Leo looks shocked. "Improvise?"

Brenda laughs softly, and it settles my nerves to see that she is unconcerned. "Don't worry, it's all perfectly above board and legitimate. Nothing will dampen the day for our two lovebirds, you have my word on that."

As we follow her downstairs, I wonder if she trained as a priest along with all her other experiences. It wouldn't surprise me because she appears to have done everything else.

We reach the library and I note the foliage decorating the doorframe and spy the mistletoe entwined around the ivy. Brenda heads inside the room and Leo stops for a moment before following her and grins rakishly, pulling me towards him, he lowers his lips to mine and I taste the future. He pulls back and whispers, "Did I tell you that you are beautiful, Scarlett?"

We hear giggling and turn to see Rebecca and Jamie standing there looking gorgeous in their wedding finery. I catch Leo's eye and feel myself blushing as he smiles sweetly and then heads inside, leaving me a hot mess to deal with. I try to look normal in front of Jamie and Rebecca but find I can't stop grinning. Wow, as days go, this day just can't get any better.

I was right.

The minutes tick by as we wait for Fiona. All the time I re-live every minute of what just happened upstairs. I feel different somehow. More alive and as if a fog has cleared and I see things clearly. I feel a shiver of desire as I think about Leo waiting on the other side of that door. How did I get so lucky? I dread to think how different things could have been if I hadn't seen that advert for Holly Island.

As the clock chimes nearby, it reminds me that we appear

to be running late. Rebecca looks worried as Jamie starts fidgeting. "It's now 2.30, and I thought the ceremony was due to start at 2 pm. Do you think everything's ok?"

Before I can think of an answer, the door opens and Brenda pokes her head around the door and looks worried. "Have you seen Fiona? What's the holdup?"

Shaking my head, I say quickly, "I'll go and see if I can find her."

However, as I turn to go, I can see there is no need for a search party because I can see her walking slowly towards us and my mouth drops to the floor. What is she wearing?

I stare in surprise as she walks towards me in MY dress. The scarlet one that I couldn't get out of my mind. Why is she wearing that? Surely the ivory one was the perfect choice; I am so confused.

I notice she looks a little weary and the alarm bells start ringing. Something's wrong.

As she draws near, Brenda says loudly, "Thank goodness for that."

She heads inside the room and I hear her shout, "Positions everyone."

I hear the music strike up a soul-searching aria that brings tears to my eyes and as Fiona reaches me, she smiles bravely. "I'm sorry I'm late."

I can tell my questions will have to wait because there is a determination in her expression that speaks volumes. Fiona is ready for whatever this is and she takes a deep breath as she places a hand on the doorway and pushes her way inside.

We follow her and I feel a sense of unease that I can't explain. I see the faces turn to stare as we make our way slowly down the short aisle to the sounds of the haunting melody. The room is silent apart from the music and I blink the tears away as I see what a fabulous job Phoebe has done. It's like a fairy tale. Flowers mix with foliage in all the splendour of nature. Fairy lights twinkle their magic and cast the room in an ethereal light. Candles burn and dance in time to the music and the yards and yards of silk and satin transform the dusty library into a magical setting.

I see the smiles on the faces of the guests as they anticipate the service and see how amazing they all look, and it's as if I've been transported to a fairy tale. Then I see Leo watching my progress and my heart beats a little faster. He is staring at me, shutting the rest of the room out and I feel the hunger in his eyes as he watches me walking towards him, knowing we are now lovers.

Then I blink in shock as I see Martin standing before the stand-in priest. I stifle a giggle as I see Harold dressed in a white sheet with Alice's sailor hat sitting proudly on top of his head as he watches the 'bride' approach.

Shaking my head, I look to my left and see Alice wearing the beautiful ivory gown, looking so beautiful I can't tear my eyes from her. She winks as I pass, and I turn to see the look in Martin's eyes as his wife draws level with him.

I study him hard because although he certainly looks handsome in his white suit with blue edging, he has that triumphant, slightly pompous expression that makes my blood run cold.

As Fiona takes her place by his side, Leo looks across at me and I can tell that he is finding this hard. He throws me a pained looked as he shakes his head slightly and then steps back to take his seat in the front row.

As Harold steps forward, I think I hold my breath as he begins by saying, "Dearly beloved, we are gathered here today to celebrate the marriage of Martin and Fiona Fellowes. They have chosen to renew those sacred vows and commit to a lifetime together forsaking all others."

He stares at the couple proudly before booming, "In the absence of the priest who was sadly unable to get here in time, I have been drafted in my Naval capacity to conduct the service."

Alice calls out, "Hear! Hear!" and he winks at her as he turns to Martin and says proudly, "Martin, have you prepared your speech?"

Martin nods and turns to face Fiona, taking her hands in his and begins earnestly. "Fiona, my love. You were always the woman for me ever since I first laid eyes on you. I knew then that you were special and would make me the happiest man alive. I would cross continents just to see your smile and fight a war to return to your side. I vow to you that I will never take our love for granted again and nurture and protect you like the delicate flower you are. I want to commit to you for eternity because there was never anyone for me but you. I want to put the past behind us and never speak of it again and move forward hand in hand, as a loving couple who will grow old together and stay married for eternity. So, Fiona, my love, my wife and the beat of my heart, will you honour me by walking with me into the future as my wife and the love of my life?"

I think the room holds its breath as all eyes turn to Fiona, who says nothing.

It's a little awkward as we wait because Martin has the same fixed look on his face that appeared as he uttered his last word. It's as if the moment is frozen in time as it waits for one word to release us from our spell and I sense the impatience and unease in the room as the words never come.

Harold steps forward and whispers, "You may answer him, dear."

Stepping back, he beams around the room, but still, the words don't come. The guests start to shift in their seats as Martin looks at Fiona and smiles reassuringly and then says gently, "What do you say, darling?"

Fiona just stares at him and then turns to face the room.

She looks a little crazy as she shakes her head and laughs dully. Then she turns back to her husband and drops his hands before saying in an emotionless voice, "Martin. There is something I need to say and now is apparently the perfect time. You may be wondering why I chose this dress when there was a much more suitable option for the occasion."

I watch Martin but he is still smiling at her, almost as if he is going to brazen out what she says next, so they can carry on regardless of it. Fiona fists the fabric of her dress and laughs. "I chose to dress like the scarlet woman I am. How could I wear white or the next best thing? I am no virgin and not that innocent as it happens. No, I am wearing scarlet to remind you of where our marriage took us. I cheated on you, Martin, and yet here you are, willing to forgive and forget so easily."

She turns to face the room and I sense the unease of the other guests. "What do you think I should do? Should I commit the rest of my life to someone who betrayed his own brother to get what he wanted?"

There's an audible gasp as she faces Martin with her eyes filled with fury. "You think I don't know about the lies you told me all those years ago just to get what you wanted. You thought that it was of no consequence to take what you wanted at the expense of two people's feelings."

Her voice breaks as Martin makes to silence her, and she pulls away. "I loved Guy, really loved him. We were engaged to be married, and I was so happy. He was the man I gave my virginity to and loved with all my heart, but you tainted it and stripped me of any love I ever had for him when you told me he cheated on me. You showed me evidence that I have since realised was fabricated. You paid a woman to tell me she had been sleeping with my fiancé to drive a wedge between us. You made me feel wanted when I was at my lowest point. You picked me up and told me everything would be ok and you would make sure of it. You wormed your way into my affections because you reminded me of him. Yes, how does it feel knowing that the only reason I went with you was because of him? The man I gave my heart to, and you pulled me away before I had the chance to get it back. Well, he did come back, and I discovered he had kept it safe all these years. He told me what you did, and I still didn't believe him. But it didn't matter anymore. What was done was done, and I left all of that in the past because only one thing mattered. I still loved him. It was inevitable that we rekindled our flame that had never really been extinguished. I knew the moment I felt his arms around me that it was always him- always Guy, but he had thrown away something special by lying and cheating - or so I thought."

She breaks off and looks across at me and smiles. "Then we came to Holly Island. I thought it would repair the damage and put some distance between Guy and myself to put me back on track. I had made my choice and needed to make things right. Then I heard you."

Her voice breaks and I notice that Martin has grown pale and his smile has slipped. She nods, "Yes, I heard you telling Scarlett about how things had worked out so well for you. You were glad that I had strayed because I would now spend my life making it up to you."

She stares at him with such hatred before spitting, "How dare you. How dare you manipulate my life like this? Well, in answer to your question, no. No, I will not walk into the future with you. I want a divorce."

We watch in horror as she rips the wedding ring off her finger and throws it to the ground before turning on her heel and fleeing from the room. Martin stares after her in disbelief before bending down and grabbing the ring and saying quickly, "Um... I think the nerves have taken hold of her. I'll go after her and calm the situation down. Stay here everyone, I won't be long."

As he runs after Fiona, the rest of us stare in stunned disbelief. Then the gentle murmurs begin until the room erupts in loud conversation as we struggle to understand how such a perfect moment can turn so sour.

Then somebody shouts, "Silence. I have something to say."

CHAPTER 36

*T*he noise in the room cuts off so quickly it's as if somebody pressed the mute button and we look in surprise to see Alice standing at the front of the room looking much more like a bride than Fiona certainly did.

As the silence covers the room in a welcome calm, she looks at Harold nervously before taking his hand and saying, "Will you marry me, Harold?"

All eyes turn to Harold, who looks so shocked it's almost comical. "Wha... what did you say?"

He shakes his head and pokes his finger in his right ear as if he's unblocking it and Alice smiles softly. "I said, will you marry me?"

Harold is speechless and you could hear a feather drop in the room as he whispers, "Why?"

Taking his hand, Alice says softly, "Because we don't have long. Because I have realised that I don't want my time with you to end. Because ever since I met you, I have been planning this moment and because I love you, Harold."

My heart splinters and the only thing holding it together

is a ray of hope as I see the tears forming in Harold's eyes. "You love – me?"

Alice nods. "I do. I thought I was happy playing around with every available man on offer. I thought it didn't matter seeing you with other women and taking them to places I wanted to go with you. When Fred died, I thought I was 'off the hook', as they say. Our marriage was nowhere near as exciting as the hours I've spent with you and it made me realise how I've wasted my life. You see, in my day, we were just grateful to meet someone and marry quickly so that we weren't left on the shelf. We were told that no life and no marriage was perfect and there was no other way but to work through your problems. Divorce was frowned upon and was never really an option. There was no room for failure in a marriage and so we had to put up and shut up. Well, I beg to differ. I am proud of Fiona for standing up for what her heart tells her. I was cheering her on inside because no woman, or man, for that matter, should settle for second best. We all have a soul mate out there waiting, and I've found mine. I don't want to lose what we have and even if we have one month, one year, or ten years, I want to spend them with you."

Her voice breaks and I don't think there's a dry eye in the house as Harold wipes the tears from his and then drops to his knees before her. "Alice Hardcastle, will you marry me?"

We all gasp as Alice smiles, "You know I will."

It takes him a while and then only because Leo helps him up, but then Harold takes Alice's hand and says loudly, "It takes a wise woman to see what is blatantly staring a man in the face. Alice saw what I should have always known. We were meant for each other. It may have taken us a lifetime to reach this point, but the only thing that matters is that we got there in the end. She asked me to marry her, but I am a proud man. No woman should have to ask something that a stupid old fool couldn't realise for himself. So, the question is mine to ask my dear because I want you to feel what it's like to be asked properly."

Alice nods and says loudly, "You stupid old fool, of course I'll marry you but remember, we all know that it was my idea in the first place."

Cheering breaks out around the room where just a few moments ago, shock and horror reigned. Now there is nothing but happiness for the two people who deserve the best happy ever after of them all.

As the noise subsides, Harold says in a worried voice, "But who can marry us? I can't perform the ceremony myself; it would be wrong."

Suddenly, Colin stands up and says loudly, "I'll do it."

We stare at him in surprise as Brenda laughs. "Yes, he doesn't like to boast about it, but Colin was ordained years before I met him. You could say I corrupted him because he gave it all up for me when I sang in the women's choir. Well, our connection was tangible, and it was inevitable that I would be the one to de-frock him."

Colin nods. "It's true. It was the right thing to do. Brenda and I have lived an amazing life together. We have travelled the world and left no opportunity unanswered. Our motto has always been to 'live each day as your last' and embrace change. We don't dwell on things that go wrong and just learn from them. The things we've seen and done would fill a thousand books. We live lives that others never consider possible and yet we are proof that the impossible is just reality waiting to happen. So, if you'll let me, I would be proud to marry you both."

Leo catches my eye and the look on his face makes me giggle. He looks for want of a better word, Flabbergasted.

As he moves across to stand beside me, his hand finds mine. Our fingers entwine as we watch a ceremony that is unexpected, unusual and so beautiful it outshines every other wedding that came before it. Alice and Harold make the perfect couple and as we witness their marriage vows, it teaches me a valuable lesson. Don't settle for anything less than the dream. You will get there in the end.

AFTER THE WEDDING, we return to the lounge, where tables have been set up with what appears to be a royal banquet. I see Marigold standing in the corner and move across to join her. "You look beautiful, Marigold. That dress really suits you."

I'm not lying because Marigold looks amazing. Her dress is the softest pink with ivory lace panels. There is a simplicity to it that's just perfect. Sometimes the most beautiful things are the natural ones, and Marigold is testament to that. She smiles happily and I note the tears in her eyes. "It's been a wonderful day, hasn't it, Scarlett. Everything has worked out well and we still have Christmas day to look forward to."

I nod but say a little sadly, "Not for Fiona and Martin, though. I wonder what will happen to them now."

Marigold shakes her head and smiles. "What was always meant to. They were never meant to be together, and that is why the cracks forced them apart. When it's the real thing, nothing can break it. Good foundations build a healthy relationship and any imperfections need to be addressed when they show themselves. If you gloss over the cracks, they will destroy you in the end."

"How did you get so wise, Marigold?"

She laughs loudly. "Years of experience, my dear. Anyway, I think we should grab some champagne and toast the happy couple."

She makes to go and I say sadly, "Should we go and see if Fiona and Martin are ok, it feels wrong celebrating when their world has just been blown apart."

Marigold shakes her head. "You won't find them my dear. If I'm not mistaken, they've left already."

"Left, but how?"

Looking out of the window, Marigold smiles. "The storm has passed, and all is now still. Ryan has taken them to shore in the boat because they needed to leave. They couldn't stay here anymore because they had much to sort out. Don't feel bad for them, Scarlett. What happened was inevitable. Maybe now they can both move on and find happiness. It's better to travel the right road than to find out that the one you're on leads to a dead end."

She heads outside the room as Leo comes over and kisses me lightly on the lips. "How soon before we can leave without it being rude?"

Giggling, I stare at the man I know I was meant to find and say in a whisper, "I'm sure nobody will miss us if we're quick."

Giggling like a couple of school kids, we race outside and return to a place we only want to be, with each other.

CHAPTER 37

I'm not sure how many times Leo and I sneak off. We grab stolen kisses and frantic hugs. We explore each other like explorers who can't believe what they have discovered. Then we return to the party and dance the night away before sneaking off and grabbing more time in the strangest places. The kitchen, the library, the vacant bedrooms and the little office. Holly Island hotel becomes our own adventure playground and I never want the night to end.

We dance to old records and I enjoy spending time with my fellow guests. I laugh at Harold spinning Alice around the floor as if they were forty years younger. I watch with a little twinge of alarm as Ryan steers Rebecca around the floor to the soft melody of a love song and don't miss the light in their eyes as they sway in gentle time to the music. I laugh when I see Jamie curled up on a settee fast asleep with Jasper snuggled up beside him and I smile as I see Phoebe and Kevin hugging by the darkened window, looking out at the stars.

Brenda and Colin are laughing and it strikes me how

lucky we were that they were here. Nothing fazes them and they have an answer for everything.

Marigold is clearing away, which makes me feel bad, so I head across to help her while Leo adds logs to the fires.

"Thanks, Scarlett, I could do with some help. It's been an amazing day, hasn't it?"

I nod, looking fondly at Alice and Harold as they sway to the music like teenagers in love. "The best. Now we have Christmas day to look forward to."

Marigold smiles and I see the excitement in her eyes. "Oh, I love Christmas, Scarlett. It's such a special time where everyone comes together and the world is a better place."

Laughing, I follow her to the kitchen, juggling the remnants of the finest wedding cake. "You're wasted here, Marigold. Maybe you should find out what the new owners of Holly Island intend on doing with the place. If they want to build a new hotel, I'm sure they will need someone on hand who knows this place inside and out."

For a moment she looks a little sad and then smiles sweetly, "Maybe; who knows, we may unwrap a Christmas miracle tomorrow."

We hear voices outside and see Phoebe carrying a sleepy dog behind Kevin, who is carrying an even sleepier child up the stairs to bed. Marigold laughs softly. "It's always lovely to spend Christmas with children and animals. We need to make Christmas day magical for them."

I nod and feel a little sad that Santa may not be as generous to Jamie this year and vow to try to make it more about the day to disguise the lack of gifts under the tree.

Once we have cleared up, I head off to find Leo, who is sitting in the lounge in one of the chairs by the fire. He's holding a glass filled with an amber liquid that catches the light of the flames as he swirls it in his hand. I grab a similar drink and join him, and he stretches out in contentment.

"Today was probably one of the best of my life thanks to you Scarlett."

Laughing, I raise my glass to him. "The first of many I hope."

Nodding, he says softly, "If I have anything to do with it, definitely."

That night, as we place our homemade gifts under the little tree that we dug out of the ground roots and all and decorated with so much love and laughter, we stand for a moment hand in hand and just stare.

"It's perfect."

Leo nods. "The best."

The clock ticks loudly as it counts down to Christmas. The fire glows with just embers as it prepares to settle down for the night and the fairy lights on the tree highlight the gaily wrapped presents beneath it.

Leo takes my hand and we head off to bed, secure in the knowledge that Christmas miracles do happen and we are living proof of that. Alice got her happy ever after and Fiona and Martin started a new journey apart. As we climb the stairs to go to bed, I wonder what the next day will bring.

CHAPTER 38

*I*t's Christmas Day.

That's the first thought that springs to mind when I open my eyes. Shaking Leo, I say with excitement, "Wake up, it's Christmas Day."

Groaning, he pulls me down and anchors me in place, saying gruffly, "You're going nowhere, let's stay here for just a few minutes more."

I snuggle into him, marvelling at how happy I feel. Yesterday was like a dream come true and I'm just glad that I've woken up to find it was real after all. I think about my friends and family waking up to Christmas for the first time without me and feel a little homesick.

My mum would have been up hours ago preparing the Christmas Turkey and adding the finishing touches, making sure that the day went by without a hitch.

My father would be rolling his eyes and complaining that Christmas was too commercial and the real message had been lost years ago, before excusing himself to head down to the pub and drown his sorrows with just about every other man on our street.

Rita will probably be still asleep after her usual Christmas Eve party, where she will snog some guy she's just met under the mistletoe. Then she will roll in in the early hours, drunkenly singing Slade's Merry Christmas amid shouts of anger from her neighbours. And Gregory. I wonder what he will be doing this Christmas? If what Rita tells me is true, he will have a different girl's name on the present he places carefully under the tree. He will hold a different hand in midnight mass and meet a different girl to help deliver the donated toys to the local children's hospital. Yes, Gregory deserves a different girl, one that will love him for his charitable ways and interest in the universe. One who will wear his annual Christmas jumper with pride and be ecstatic about spending the New Year camping on Dartmoor. Gregory deserves the very best because he is a special person, just not my special person. No, the man I was always meant to find just needs to free himself from his current situation before we can ride off into the sunset together.

Thinking about Davina, I wonder what her Christmas day will be like. I feel a prickle of doubt settle on my mind as I wonder about the truth behind Leo's words. Is it really a non-starter, as he said it was, or are they really lovers and best friends and I'm getting in the way of something special?

I can't seem to shake off the alarm that's threatening to burst my bubble and say quickly, "Leo."

"Hmm."

"Um… just a silly thought, but, um… well, Davina won't really be upset when you return home with me – will she?"

He opens his eyes immediately and says quickly, "Of course not. Why?"

"It's just that now it's Christmas Day. I don't like to think of her sad and lonely without you. What if she's really upset and I'm some kind of happiness wrecker? I couldn't bear it if

I thought I was splitting up a couple where at least one of them was in love."

Leo bursts out laughing and pulls me close, kissing me furiously. Then he pulls back and looks me in the eye and says firmly, "I was never dating Davina."

"But you said…"

"No, I said my father wanted me to. I'm not going to pretend we haven't been out on the odd date or two. Usually when she needed someone to accompany her to an event, but we were just friends. No, she was invited this Christmas so that I could turn it around and ask her out properly. My father wanted me to make it official and I expect she was dreading it as much as me."

"Why?"

He laughs and his mouth twitches as he says, "Davina prefers women. She always has, but won't tell her family. I've no doubt she would have gone along with the engagement, even the marriage, if it meant keeping her family happy, as well as her trust fund. However, Davina was never interested in me in that way and is just too scared to tell the truth because she cares what people think."

I stare at him in shock. "But that's not different these days. It's accepted. Why would she hide her sexuality?"

"Just the same as why I considered asking her to marry me. The world may have moved on, but our families haven't. They are old money with old values. I'm afraid it will take the current generation to bear the burden of breaking the mould and it's a huge responsibility. How do you think my family will react when I tell them I don't want to work in the family business and instead I want to travel the world writing erotic romance?"

I start to giggle and he laughs. "What will happen when Davina comes to her senses and introduces her family to her girlfriend? They won't be able to deal with it and because we love our families above everything, neither one of us wants to be the one to damage their world. The trouble is, I will do anything to be with you, Scarlett and I'm sure when they meet you, they will love you just as much as I do. It may just take them a while to come to that conclusion."

I feel a little worried now, thinking of the hate heading my way, and Leo strokes my face lovingly and says softly, "But we don't have to worry about that. It's Christmas Day and our lives begin now - together. When we leave Holly Island, we leave as a couple and nothing will stand in the way of that."

He kisses me so lovingly any doubts are immediately erased. Who cares what the rest of the world thinks? We will deal with that when it happens. Until then, we will just enjoy our first Christmas as a couple in this magical place.

AFTER A WHILE, we get dressed and head downstairs. Hearing laughter coming from the lounge, we grin and head off to see what the fuss is about. Barking greets us as we push the door open, and I stare in amazement at the sight before me.

Jamie is sitting by the fireplace surrounded by boxes and boxes of opened presents. Rebecca is laughing at Jasper, who is tearing up a ball of paper nearby. Phoebe and Kevin are smiling happily, and they look up as we step inside the room. "Happy Christmas, guys."

"Happy Christmas, it looks as if Santa's been Jamie."

He shouts happily, "Look, Scarlett. Santa found me and I wasn't on the naughty list. He's bought me everything I wanted and I can't believe it."

I catch Phoebe's eye and she nods towards Rebecca, who is ruffling Jasper's fur lovingly. As Leo picks up one of the toys that need assembling, I sit beside Phoebe and she whispers, "Apparently, Rebecca enlisted Ryan's help and sent him to the mainland to buy the things on Jamie's list. They kept them at his mother's cottage and wrapped them in secret."

I look across at Rebecca in amazement as Phoebe's eyes fill with tears. "I can't believe she did this for Jamie – for us. I never even knew she realised there was a problem. We've been so careful to keep it from the children and now she's done something so amazing."

Looking across at Rebecca helping Jamie with a puzzle, I say thoughtfully, "She's not a child anymore, she's a young adult. I think she notices a lot more than you think. I also think she's struggling to find where she fits in between two families. Maybe this is her way of doing just that and she wants to help."

Phoebe nods and looks thoughtful as Brenda enters the room and claps her hands. "Attention please, attention please."

We look up in surprise and she smiles happily. "Happy Christmas, everyone from Colin and me. We would both like to say that we have very much enjoyed getting to know you all and will look back on this Christmas with fond memories. Now, I think it's time to start the ball rolling, so breakfast will be served in the dining room, courtesy this morning of Colin and I. Ryan and Marigold are the guests of honour today and will be treated accordingly."

We all nod in agreement and as we follow her out, Leo slips his hand in mine and kisses me on the cheek. "Happy Christmas, Scarlett."

"Same to you. I wonder where we'll be this time next year?"

He looks thoughtful. "Who knows but wherever it is, we'll be there together, I'm sure of that at least."

CHAPTER 39

*A*fter breakfast, we are summoned to the lounge to open the presents under the tree. I feel very excited to see what Leo thinks of his and look with interest at the gaily wrapped packages that were made here in the hotel.

Jamie is asked to be Santa's Elf and distribute the presents, guided by Brenda.

Soon we have quite a pile and I start to unwrap them eagerly.

As I unwrap the gifts, I take great delight in all of them. I have a face scrub from Rebecca and a bottle of homemade rosemary flavoured olive oil from Alice and Harold. Marigold and Ryan have given me a box of chocolate truffles wrapped in the most delightful little box. Brenda and Colin have made a lovely decoration out of twigs and sewn some scented hearts to the top of it, and I feel a pang when I see a lovely set of personalised notepaper that was left from Fiona and Martin. Phoebe and Kevin have made a lovely strawberry-flavoured gin that sits looking pretty in a fancy glass bottle tied with a ribbon.

Leo hands me a small package and looks a little worried

as I take it eagerly. "I hope you like it. I wanted to give you something of value to mark the occasion."

I feel intrigued as I gently unwrap the gift. It contains a small box and as I open it, I see a small pebble from the beach. It feels smooth and very tactile and I notice that Leo has painted our initials entwined in a love heart. When I turn it over, I see a dainty picture of Holly Island drawn beautifully on the other side, and I stare at it in amazement. "Did you do this?"

He looks a little sheepish. "No, I'm not very good at drawing. Phoebe helped me when I took her class and did most of it, if I'm honest. I just wanted something personal that you could take with you and always remember this Christmas. Do you like it?"

I nod. "I love it. It's very thoughtful and I'll always treasure it."

Shyly, I hand him the parcel I wrapped for him. "It's not much but I hope you like it."

He grins with excitement as he opens it and pulls out the little painting I did of Holly Island. Unlike his, mine is in colour and drawn on an old piece of material that I found in the attic. Ryan helped me nail it to some strips of wood to make a canvas and I've signed and dated the bottom.

He smiles and leans over and kisses me softly. "I love it. I will hang it in pride of place in my apartment."

As we swap gifts with our newfound friends and enjoy the simplicity of a usually commercially filled day, it strikes me that I've never been as happy as I am now. It doesn't matter that we have no television to watch. It's quite liberating not to have to field the telephone calls and texts of various friends and relatives and it's absolutely lovely to receive meaningful gifts that cost nothing to make from people who have put so much thought into them. Most of all, though, I have found the most precious gift of all and he is sitting beside me.

We sit for a while, just swapping stories and laughing and joking with our friends. There is no urgency to fit everything in. The atmosphere is relaxed and exactly as I always imagined it to be in a perfect world.

Then the moment we have all been waiting for comes and we head to the kitchen to help Brenda and Colin bring in the Christmas dinner. Everybody takes a dish into the dining room and places it on a long table that has been set up the length of the room. Today, there are no individual tables. We will all eat together and share the most important meal of the year.

Harold insists on carving the Turkey and Leo makes sure that everybody has a drink. Ryan entertains Rebecca and Jamie and, as I watch them, I feel a little sad. In two days' time, we will all leave and I wonder what that will mean for him. He appears to enjoy Rebecca's company and I wish they could keep in touch. Maybe they will and who knows, something may come of it. I certainly hope so.

I sit between Phoebe and Leo and as we tuck into the amazing dinner Brenda and Colin have provided, I say with interest, "Have you thought anymore about starting up as an event planner?"

She nods and I see the excitement in her eyes that wasn't there before. "Yes, as it happens, Brenda has a contact that may be interested in helping me."

Brenda overhears our conversation and says, "Yes, after that beautiful display she put on yesterday, it got me thinking. I have a friend who designs events for celebrities. I met him when I worked on the OK weddings that I told you about. Well, we kept in touch and I thought of him yesterday. He is in so much demand that he turns work away, so I thought he may be interested in working with Phoebe. He provides the contacts and she will run the events. I'm sure they could work it out between them; I'll set up a meeting when we get home."

I say in surprise, "That's great news, you must be ecstatic."

Phoebe nods. "I am. Maybe it will help us if Kevin loses his job. If he doesn't, the money will make all the difference to our future."

Kevin leans over and smiles. "I've been telling her for years she should set up a business. She's always thrown the best parties for Jamie and helped her friends with theirs. I think she'll be very good at it."

He looks thoughtful. "Even if I do lose my job, I'm not one to worry about it. There are other things I can do and we'll muddle through."

Suddenly, Rebecca says loudly, "Well, you won't have to pay my university fees anymore."

Silence falls as everyone looks at her in surprise and I notice that Kevin turns as white as a sheet. "Why?"

She shrugs. "Because I'm not going back."

Phoebe looks worried and Jamie says in a worried voice. "I didn't tell anyone, Becca."

She smiles at him fondly. "I know you didn't JJ. You're a good keeper of secrets which is why Santa gave you so many presents."

Jamie nods looking very proud of himself and Phoebe says faintly, "I think you had better explain, darling."

Rebecca nods and looks across at Harold and grins. I feel as if a storm is about to break and I hold my breath as she smiles happily. "Well, it may come as a surprise to you all but Harold and I have been meeting in secret."

There's an awkward silence and I try hard not to make eye contact with anyone because this is weird. Harold laughs loudly. "Yes, we've had such fun tiptoeing around hiding our secret meetings from you all but it was worth it, I think."

Rebecca nods as Kevin says in a strangled voice, "Please get to the point, Rebecca."

She nods. "Well, Harold has been helping me with a decision I've been thinking about for some time now and Ryan has helped make it happen."

This time we all look at Ryan who nods. "It was my pleasure."

I think Kevin is about to have a heart attack as the tension builds and then Rebecca blurts out, "I'm going to join the Navy."

For a moment, nothing happens. We all just stare at her and try to understand what that means. Jamie looks excited and says, "I heard Becca talking about it with Ryan. They said she would go to sea and everything. I can't wait to visit the ship and she said she would show me around."

Rebecca laughs, "Of course I will. Just as soon as I'm assigned one. We have filled in the application form and I have an interview booked for the 5th January."

Kevin suddenly says in a very firm voice. "No."

Phoebe appears to shrink back in her seat as Rebecca yells, "What do you mean - no? I can do what I want, I'm 19 nearly 20 for god's sake. I can do what I like and don't need you or anyone else to tell me otherwise."

Kevin turns to Phoebe and shouts, "Tell her, tell her it's madness. Why would a beautiful young girl want to go to sea and fight wars? Why would a young, impressionable, girl want to surround herself with men with one-track minds on a ship for months on end?"

Alice looks excited and nods at Rebecca approvingly and I must admit I can see the appeal of it myself put like that. Rebecca, however, rolls her eyes and then says in a gentle voice, "I'm sorry dad, this must be quite a shock."

"A shock. It's much more than just a shock, it's total madness. What would your mother say? No, you haven't thought this through, darling. You can't just throw away your education on a whim like this, it would be irresponsible of me as your father to allow it!"

Rebecca looks at him sadly and I think even the clouds outside stop scuttling to take a look. "I'm not your little girl anymore, dad. Somewhere along the line I grew up and struggled to find my way. University isn't for me, in fact, I hate every minute of it. I'm going through the motions because I don't know any different. I can't remember the last time I saw mum and when I did, she was already packing for her next trip. You try your best but you have a new family and as hard as you try, I don't feel as if I fit in. My friends are all scattered around the country, either working or at university and as the time marches on I have less and less in common with them. I'm not even sure what I'll do with my degree when I get it because political science bores me rigid. No, I have been miserable for some time now and when I saw the advert for the Navy something sparked inside me. I discovered more and the more I learned the more I liked. It's not all about fighting and going off to war. There are many job roles within it and room to progress. No, my mind is made up and I'm doing this with, or without, your blessing because ultimately this is my life and I need to take charge of it."

I think I'm about to cry as I see the sadness surrounding Rebecca and the expression on Kevin's face. He looks destroyed.

Phoebe puts her hand on his arm and I see the pity mixed with something else on her face. There's a determination in her eyes as she looks at Rebecca and says softly, "I think you're amazing, Rebecca. I know you feel awkward around me and I understand that. I'm not your mother and never will be but I am your friend. I think the only thing that matters here is that you are happy. We all start off in life doing things we think we want to and it takes a brave person to stand up and change direction midway. It's obvious that a lot of thought has gone into this and if you wouldn't mind, maybe you can explain it all to us later and we can understand what it involves. You have my full support and I'm sure when he gets his head around it, you will have your father's too."

"You have mine, Becca. I can't wait to see your uniform." Jamie yells and we all laugh.

Harold looks a little bemused and says loudly, "It was the best decision I ever made. Loved every minute of it and we didn't have half the opportunities these kids do. Goodness, the things they get to do these days. If I had my time again, I'd do exactly the same thing. I must say, I've enjoyed every minute of our discussions, young lady and I wish you well. It feels a little strange, women being in the Navy but I can't see why not; it makes for a more interesting voyage at least."

Alice nudges him and smiles at Rebecca. "I think you're very lucky dear. If I had my time again, I would jump on board. There's no reason why a woman can't join the Navy, the uniform is the better one and navy and white is so flattering. Yes, I'm quite envious really, good luck to you."

Brenda nods. "It reminds me of the time we were stranded at sea when our yacht developed a technical problem. Do you remember that American frigate that came to our rescue, Colin? My, my, what an experience that was. I haven't drunk so much again - ever. I'm with you, Rebecca, an admirable career path and, if I may say so, the right one for someone who feels as if they need a centre to their life, a family and a purpose. Good luck darling, you will be amazing."

Kevin looks a little shamefaced and I watch him battle with his emotions. It feels a little awkward because, on the one hand, we all want to congratulate Rebecca but it's obvious Kevin disapproves. Then he sighs and I'm shocked to see the tears in his eyes, as he says gruffly, "I'm sorry, Becca, you're right. It's just that when I see you, I see the little girl I tucked in and read bedtime stories. I see that little girl who skipped along the road to school and proudly brought her paintings home to show me. I see the baby I never believed I'd feel so much love for and I see the little girl I let down when my marriage broke up. I have only ever wanted the best for you, despite what you may have thought. It scares me to death to think of you out there on your own without me to hold your hand. It worries me thinking of you so far from home with no way of getting to you if you need me. But most of all, it scares me to think that the distance that grows between us will be of my own doing because, despite my fears, I want you to know that I am always here for you. So, I'm proud of you, darling and you have my full support and when we get home, I'll be beside you every step of the way and will be the proudest father at your passing out parade."

There's not a dry eye around the table as he scrapes his chair back and moves over to hug his daughter. As she sobs with relief in his arms, I feel happy for them both. They have reached a place where they can start to build a different kind of relationship. The one where the parent recognises their child has become an adult and adopts a different role. Kevin should be very proud of his daughter because she has grown up to be an amazing young woman.

CHAPTER 40

*S*omehow, we all pull ourselves together and carry on enjoying Christmas dinner. When I look around me, it's obvious that since coming here, things have changed for the people at this table. Holly Island hasn't just touched my life, it's touched every person's here and I can't wait to start my adventure with Leo and vow to keep in touch with every last one of my fellow guests.

Once lunch is over, we all help tidy up and then retire to the lounge and make sure to keep our glasses topped up all afternoon while playing charades and putting on the show that Brenda organised when we first came. The more we drink; the crazier things get, and I haven't laughed so much in years.

Gradually, though, people drift away either to grab a much-needed siesta, or to enjoy alone time with their loved ones. Leo and I decide to take a walk to try to shift some of the Christmas pudding, and it feels so good to walk with his hand in mine as we head toward the sea.

The air is crisp and cold and the sun shines brightly in the sky. The sea sparkles like the brightest light on the Christmas tree and the ground is cold and hard beneath our feet.

Our breath forms little clouds as it freezes in the air and the birds chatter excitedly around us.

As we stand and look out to sea, Leo pulls me close against his side and says gently, "Thank you. This has been the best Christmas I've ever had and I'm looking forward to spending every other one with you."

His words light up my soul and I feel a little tingle of excitement as I nod happily. "This is the beginning, isn't it, Leo?"

"The beginning?"

"Yes, it may be the end of one story. Like all romances, they usually end at this point in the book. The two lovers have found each other and the 'Happy Ever After' is guaranteed. This is where the story leaves them as they ride off into the sunset together, but now a different story starts."

Laughing softly, Leo nods. "I never thought about it like that, but you're right. Yes, the story of how we met and fell in love is done and dusted, but there is a much more interesting story waiting to be told. It's the one where they go on to live a happy, fulfilled life with many adventures waiting to be experienced. Take Brenda and Colin, for instance. Their life is spent just moving from one adventure to the other. I hope that's us. I don't want to settle for just ordinary when there is extraordinary out there. Let's be that couple. Let's experience life, not just live it."

Laughing, he spins me around and we fall to the ground in a heap, laughing. Then he pulls me close and kisses me hard and fast and despite the cold ground and the icy wind that blows, I feel warm inside. Like Rebecca, I found my direction, and it feels amazing.

BOXING DAY DAWNS and it's a much more subdued affair. I suppose in the back of our minds, we know that it's our last day on the island and it's bittersweet.

After breakfast, Leo and I head out for a walk with Phoebe and Jamie and enjoy watching Jasper play with whatever he finds. We all laugh at the little dog and I feel sad thinking they may have to leave him. Phoebe laughs as Jamie chases him and says happily, "I love seeing him so happy. It's all a mother wants really, to see her child content and loving life."

Leo laughs. "He's a credit to you both. I don't envy you tomorrow, though, when you have to say your goodbyes to Jasper."

She grins. "We won't. Kevin agreed that Jasper can come home with us. No amount of money could buy the happiness that dog gives us. We can afford a few pounds a week to buy him some food. So what if we have to go without to pay for his vet's bills? It's a small sacrifice to make when you think about the joy he will bring to our family."

My heart lifts and I smile as I hear the joyful bark of the puppy and the laughter of the small boy chasing him. "I'm glad you're giving him a home. I think it's the right thing to do."

Phoebe nods. "You know, we are leaving Holly Island as a much tighter family than the one that arrived. Rebecca and I have reached an understanding and are friends more than anything. She knows I would never try to take her mother's place, and yet she is just as much a part of this family as any of us. Along with Jamie, she is the centre of it and I think she knows that now. Kevin has been forced to admit that she has grown up, and he needs to let her go in order to keep her. Their relationship will just develop stronger ties of a different kind. Jamie is happy because he has a new friend to play with and I have an exciting new opportunity to sink my teeth into when we return. I'm so happy we came and yet excited to leave, but I want us all to stay in touch and maybe you can come and visit us when you get the chance."

Leo and I nod and he says warmly, "We will. You can count on that. Like you, I am so glad I took a chance and came because if I didn't, I would never have met Scarlett. When I leave, it's with the woman I love and what can be better than that?"

Phoebe smiles and looks interested. "So, what now for the two of you; what are your plans?"

I look at Leo and he smiles. "Well, I hope that once we've visited Scarlett's family, she will come and meet mine. I do have an apartment in London we can use as a base and once I've wrapped things up with work, I'm hoping we can arrange a trip together."

I interrupt. "I still need to find a job though, so at first I'll just take what I can until we decide what we're doing. It's exciting though because we have a blank sheet waiting to be filled. There is no grand plan to follow, just an exciting world of possibilities to explore."

Jamie comes rushing up and yells, "Mummy, it's snowing."

We all look up in surprise and see that he's right. From out of nowhere, the snow has begun to fall and as we feel the light, soft, flakes, touch our lips, we smile in delight. Jamie shouts, "I hope it snows a lot so we can make a snowman; do you think it will?"

Phoebe laughs. "I doubt it, darling. It will take a lot of snow for that to happen."

As Leo's hand finds mine, we look in wonder at one of nature's miracles as it starts to cover the frosty ground with a white blanket. Jamie and Jasper run around trying to catch the flakes of powder and it feels as if there is magic everywhere.

By the time we return to the hotel, there is quite a

covering on the ground. After stamping the snow off four pairs of boots, we head to the kitchen in search of warming mugs of hot chocolate and by the time we take them to the library, there is a different type of light shining in from the window.

Leo looks out and laughs softly. "I think Jamie will get his wish because it's a blizzard out there and the snow is settling fast."

Joining him, I watch the steam from my drink cover the window.

The view outside looks just like a Christmas card, framed by the leaded window panes. The branches are filled with snow and the ground a white powder blanket. All around us is the silence that snow brings with it as it covers the beauty of nature's garden with magic.

Our last day on Holly Island was spent building Jamie's snowman.

Our last day was filled with lots of laughter and our last day was tinged with sadness because, for Holly Island at least, this could be the end of one story and the beginning of a new one.

Only time will tell what the future holds for any of us, this island included, but whatever that will be, there will be a future and it's up to us to make it a good one.

CHAPTER 41

$\mathcal{W}$ith a sinking feeling, I take one last look at my room and sigh. I'll miss this place and the people who shared it with me.

"Are you ready, Scarlett?"

Leo waits by the door with his own belongings all packed and ready to go and I nod. "I think so. It's hard though."

He comes over and takes my hand and squeezes it softly. "It's always hard saying goodbye to something you love. I wish I could say we'll be back, but that's unlikely. However, we will always have the memories, they can never be taken from us."

"And I have you."

I reach up and kiss him lightly on the lips, and he smiles. "And you have me."

I pick up my small bag and, after one last look, follow him downstairs.

It was hard saying goodbye to everyone earlier. Phoebe, Kevin, Rebecca, Jamie and Jasper were the first to leave after breakfast. Then it was Alice and Harold, followed an hour later by Brenda and Colin. Now it's our turn, and as I see

Marigold waiting by the entrance, I feel a lump in my throat as I realise this is goodbye.

Stifling the sob forming deep inside, I face her with a bravery that comes from somewhere and hug her warmly. "Thank you so much, Marigold. You have made this a magical experience and I will never forget you."

She hugs me back and whispers, "Take care of yourself, Scarlett, you're a good girl and will do well in life."

She turns to Leo and hugs him just as warmly and smiles, "Take care of her and be happy, both of you."

I feel worried for her and Ryan and make to speak, but she shakes her head. "Don't feel bad for us, Scarlett. I know what you're thinking and there's no need. We are happy and always will be. Life may deal a low punch from time to time, but I wouldn't change a thing. Now go, before you lose the tide and remember to always think of us fondly."

"But we must swap numbers. Maybe if you come to London you can look us up."

She laughs softly, "If it makes you feel any better, of course, I'll take your number and who knows, maybe we will meet up again one day."

As I write the number down in the guest book in the hallway, Marigold says firmly, "Now go, both of you and have a very happy New Year together."

She ushers us out, and it all happens in such a rush; I don't even get to say what I wanted to say.

As we walk away from Holly Island hotel, I take a long look back and commit it to memory. Marigold waves from the doorway and I feel bad that I never got to say goodbye to Ryan.

However, as we near the jetty, I am surprised to see Ryan's boat waiting, and he laughs at our expressions.

"Jump on board, I'll be your taxi driver today."

I stare at him in surprise as Leo throws him our bags and

then helps me into the boat. As he unties the rope and jumps in, Leo grins.

"What's this, the VIP treatment?"

Ryan grins. "Something like that."

Leo turns to me and laughs. "It looks as if we'll never get to see the departure boat."

I nod and feel a little disappointed about that. Maybe it's because it was the last puzzle of Holly Island that will remain unsolved and I want the whole experience, but having Ryan to see us off is no hardship.

Ryan's boat is far superior to Hagrid lookalike's boat, anyway, and as we skim across the water, I turn and take one last, lingering look at Holly Island. Leo notices my expression and pulls me beside him as we watch an island disappear from view that has come to mean so much to us.

"Do you think we will ever be back?" I say sadly.

Ryan interrupts. "Don't look back in life, Scarlett, just move forward. There's a lot to see out there and not enough time to do it. There are many Holly Islands out there every bit a special as this one. Find them all and discover their delights and live each day as if it's your last."

Turning to face him, I say with interest, "What about you and your mum; what does the future hold for you?"

"Who knows, more of the same maybe? Holly Island will always be here, Scarlett and we will always have a connection to it."

He breaks off as we near the jetty and it feels as if it's been months, not weeks, since we were here last. I feel a pang as I realise our journey has now officially ended and with a heavy heart, accept Leo's hand as he helps me step to shore. Our luggage soon follows and Ryan smiles happily. "There, all safely deposited back to normality. It's been lovely to meet you both and make sure you live a happy life together."

We both say our goodbyes and watch as he sets off back

the way he came, waving madly and Leo says gruffly, "I'll miss him and Marigold. In fact, I'll miss the whole crazy bunch of them."

"Then allow me to introduce you to my family if you like the crazies. You are still happy with that, aren't you?"

He spins around and pulls me close, whispering, "You're stuck with me I'm afraid and if it's crazy people you hang out with, then that's fine by me, especially if they are anything like you."

As Leo kisses me, everything falls into place. My life now has meaning and direction. It's funny how things work out when you are at your lowest point. As long as you believe and step outside your comfort zone, you may discover something you never thought you'd find.

As he pulls back, Leo grins. "Maybe we should grab a drink in the pub over there and call for a taxi to the airport."

I smile broadly. "I'm not going to argue with that."

We pull our cases behind us and head towards the old English pub that sits proudly by the dockside. It feels strange pushing the old, oak, door open because the sounds of normal life are all around us. People are laughing and joking and having a post-Christmas drink and we have to fight our way to the bar.

It takes a while before we're served and as we order our drinks, the bartender says with interest, "What brings you here to these parts? You're not local because I think I know every person who lives here."

Leo says loudly, "We're on our way back from Holly Island. I don't suppose you have the number for a local taxi company. We need a ride to the airport?"

The man nods and slides a business card across the bar and looks confused. "Holly Island, you say. Not much to see there."

Leo shakes his head. "It was amazing. We had a really good time."

Something about the way he looks at us confuses me and I say, "Why, what makes you say that?"

"Because Holly Island is just a legend. Don't get me wrong, it was once an amazing place, but after the disaster, well…"

"Well, what?" I stare at Leo in horror as the bartender shakes his head. "About twenty years ago, a terrible storm blew up and when I say terrible, it was the worst the area had ever seen. People were told to evacuate, but the people on Holly Island didn't have time. A freak tidal wave destroyed the island and everyone with it. Terrible it was, it was completely annihilated and all that's left today are the stories."

I need to sit down as Leo says in disbelief, "Stories?"

Nodding, the Bartender fumbles underneath the counter and draws out a scrapbook and pushes it across the bar. "Yes, many people come here looking for Holly Island. Legend has it that they are invited by the spirits, and many visitors have spoken about taking a boat there and staying on the island. Of course, there's no such thing because these waters are busy ones and if Holly Island was still there, we would know about it. Many people come to search for its remains. There's talk of treasure on there that's been lost forever. Divers, day-trippers and even television crews comb these waters for one glimpse of the place that lies at the bottom of the sea."

As Leo slides the money across the bar, he says, "I expect you found nothing, just like the rest."

He heads off to serve another customer, and I stare at Leo in total shock. "He can't be right; Holly Island is as real as you and me."

We grab the scrapbook and head to a table in the corner of the pub and open the pages. Before us are old photographs of the place we have just visited. It's exactly as we remember, the hotel, the gardens and even the rickety old wheelbarrow rusting by the path. Leo points to a picture of a couple standing in the doorway and I gasp. "Marigold."

I peer a little closer and see a man that looks a lot like Ryan with his arm around her and two small boys standing in front of them. The tears fill my eyes as we read the text below the photograph.

Mr and Mrs Hinchley and their sons Edward and Ryan, the caretakers of Holly Island hotel.

As we scroll through the pages, we see another newspaper cutting, but this time an obituary.

It is with great sadness that Mrs Marigold Hinchley mourns the loss of her husband Robert, after his short battle with cancer.

We can't turn the pages quickly enough as we devour the text and photographs that appear. There's one of Ryan and the text states that Marigold Hinchley of Holly Island was happy to attend the graduation of her son Ryan as he passed his veterinary exams.

It also shows a picture of his brother, which must be years later, and I almost can't speak as I point to the photograph. "It's… Hagrid!"

Leo looks stunned as we see the man who took us to Holly Island in his boat and then we read the text in disbelief. It states that following the death of his younger brother and mother in the terrible storm that devastated Holly Island, he set up a boat hire company but sadly died of cancer five years later. He had been travelling at the time of the freak accident but never got over the loss of his family.

Then there are the articles about the legend of Holly Island. Various visitors claiming to have stayed on the Island and been guests of the Hinchleys. Apparently, Edward would emerge from the fog and take the visitors to the deserted hotel where they reported staying until his brother took them home. There are various articles about possible sightings and locals backing up the visitor's stories. However, no proof has ever been found and now the stories are dismissed as hoaxes, which has given rise to the legend of Holly Island.

Leo and I just stare at the scrapbook in total disbelief. This can't be happening. It is real; of course, it is.

We sit side by side in the little alcove of the pub and normal life carries on around us. Neither one of us can comprehend what's just happened and then Leo says, "What are you thinking, Scarlett?"

I shake my head. "I don't know what to think. Either I have been drugged and just spent the night in an alley somewhere and had these amazing dreams, or something so magical just happened to us that cannot be explained."

Leo leans back and breathes out heavily. "There must surely be a rational explanation for this. Maybe someone is playing tricks on us. Perhaps this is just something the locals have made up to attract visitors here."

I close the book and nod firmly. "Of course it is. It can be nothing else. We're not mad, Leo, far from it, and we both know what we've experienced for the last two weeks. Yes, you're absolutely right, it's all part of a big tourist trap and we nearly fell for it."

I take a massive slug of my drink and reach for my phone. "Where's that number? I'll call us a cab."

As I dial the number, I let my head overrule my heart for my own sanity. Yes, Holly Island was as real as I am and all these tales of magic and fantasy are just that - tales. Marigold and Ryan are as real as Hagrid and we have just been part of a fantastic pretence.

The taxi soon arrives and as we return the book to the bartender, he smiles his thanks. "I hope to see you around these parts again someday."

Leo shakes his head. "Maybe, but Scarlett and I have a world to discover. Someone once told us to never look back. Well, it was good advice and we intend on doing just that."

He takes my hand and as we walk out into the fresh air, says happily, "Well, whatever just happened, you and I are real enough. Come on, let's go home."

We place our bags in the back of the taxi and snuggle up on the back seat as the driver says, "Where to?"

"The airport please." Leo turns and smiles, saying, "To the rest of our lives, Scarlett. May every day be as amazing as the last."

As we drive away from the quayside, I wonder what just happened. Then again, I've always believed in fairy tales and that's just what I got and sitting beside me is definitely my, 'Happily Ever After.'

Yes, surely everyone believes in fairy stories – don't they?

Thank you for reading.
I hope you enjoyed this story. If you are still in the mood for Christmas you may like Christmas in Dream Valley.
Check it out here.

I LOVE Christmas so much I have dedicated a page to it on my website. Check out my other books here

THANK you for reading Holly Island.

If you liked it, I would love if you could leave me a review, as I must do all my own advertising.

This is the best way to encourage new readers and I appreciate every review I can get. Please also recommend it to your friends as word of mouth is the best form of advertising. It won't take longer than two minutes of your time, as you only need write one sentence if you want to.

Have you checked out my website? Subscribe to keep updated with any offers or new releases.

sjcrabb.com

WHEN YOU VISIT MY WEBSITE, you may be surprised because I don't just write Romantic comedy.

I also write under the pen names M J Hardy & Harper Adams. I send out a monthly newsletter with details of all my releases and any special offers but aside from that, you don't hear from me very often.

If you like social media, please follow me on mine where I am a lot more active and will always answer you if you reach out to me.

Why not take a look and see for yourself and read Lily's Lockdown, a little scene I wrote to remember the madness when the world stopped and took a deep breath?

Lily's Lockdown

Carry on reading for more books.

MORE BOOKS BY S J CRABB

sjcrabb.com

STAY IN TOUCH

You can also follow me on social media below.

Facebook

Instagram

Twitter

Website

Bookbub

Amazon